Tom Hood

A Golden Heart

Vol. 3

Tom Hood

A Golden Heart
Vol. 3

ISBN/EAN: 9783337053734

Printed in Europe, USA, Canada, Australia, Japan

Cover: Foto ©Andreas Hilbeck / pixelio.de

More available books at **www.hansebooks.com**

A GOLDEN HEART.

𝔄 𝔑𝔬𝔳𝔢𝔩.

BY

TOM HOOD.

IN THREE VOLUMES.

VOL. III.

LONDON:

TINSLEY BROTHERS, 18 CATHERINE ST., STRAND.

1867.

WYMAN AND SONS, PRINTERS,
GREAT QUEEN STREET, LINCOLN'S INN FIELDS,
LONDON, W.C.

CONTENTS OF VOL. III.

CHAPTER I.

LOWER YET!

POOR Alice's life is becoming very lonely now, and bitter remorse and the anguish of disappointed trust are playing sad havoc with her once lovely face. The grace of her figure is gone, for she droops like a flower that has been beaten to earth by the storm. And the springiness of her step is lost, and the music has died out of her voice as the glory seems faded from her golden hair.

She sees but little of Captain Cormack now. What were all his vows and protestations and oaths worth? Now he did not think it worth his while to take the trouble to perjure himself any longer. He

III.   B

was weary of her, and did not care to conceal it from her.

She had seen his growing indifference, and her love had seemed to increase as his diminished; for I fear at first she had really cared but little for him. But it is part of the contradictory nature of woman that she should love the man who has wronged her; and now Alice seemed to feel that her whole life was staked upon his faith and affection.

Then came the dreadful awakening!

He stayed from her weeks and months at a time, and did not condescend to explain his absence. She grew jealous, and then he did not take the trouble to disguise from her that she had reason to be jealous.

Her heart was growing hard now, but yet she suffered terribly. For he was all the world to her—not in the sense that he had been in the time of her humiliation and distress. He was all the world to her now, because of the desolation he had brought round her. She had no tie in the world save her unhappy relation to him. She had no friend in the world but the man who had been her worst enemy, and who was severing even that bitter bond, and becoming utterly indifferent.

She saw no one now save the French *danseuse*, who occasionally visited her, and sometimes brought with her a lady friend, who was English by birth, and dropped her " h's" like a Briton, and who, when pressed to take some refreshment, pronounced in favour of " a little neat gin."

Alice did not like her English friend, but the French woman won upon her greatly. She was a clever woman, this opera dancer, as she described herself to be, and could talk French philosophy in a convincing manner, and without revealing the cloven foot too startlingly. Her company was a sort of moral dram-drinking for Alice, who found a temporary refuge from remorse and grief in the brilliant sophistries and wicked worldly wisdom of Mademoiselle Rosalie.

And did Rosalie care for her " dear young friend, *cette chère Alix ?* " I fear not ; for she was a very old friend of Henry Cormack's, and it was at his instigation that she had first sought to make Alice's acquaintance in order to poison her mind and lure her towards the evil snares that he was setting for her soul. Nay, even now she was working upon Alice to serve the Captain's purpose.

Was Rosalie so fond of Henry Cormack?
Not a bit, nor had she ever cared for him.
But she would do a good deal for any one
who would give her a new shawl or a new
dress; and, moreover, having sunk herself,
she was only too ready to help to drag
others down.   Now, though she was a
thoroughly bad woman, one might have
forgiven her almost anything but that; for
if a woman who has been deceived by the
man she trusted becomes hard and cruel,
and revenges upon the race wrongs inflicted
by the individual, we must not wonder
greatly; but that she should find a delight
in casting down a sister into the jaws of
destruction, is wickedness unaccountable.
It is leaguing with those who have wronged
her, and whom she desires to punish.   It is
the very perversity of wickedness.

Alice confided all her troubles to Rosalie,
little supposing that her affectionate con-
fidante was a mere spy.

One day she had been complaining more
bitterly than usual of the neglect with which
Henry Cormack had treated her for many
months.

"And he won't write a line, even though
I have begged him to do so over and over

again. And I owe for my rent, and I haven't a penny to pay it with."

" But," said her friend with a shrug, " what will you? A man cannot be ' eternally constant' for ever!"

" Ah, yes—if he really loved "——

" Bah! Loved! But is it not incredible that this girl, so old, is not yet aware that men cannot love!"

" Not love, Rosalie!"

" Certainly—without doubt. It is that which I have stated. Men can desire, can admire, can caress, can make a great deal of—but to love, oh, no! my dear Alice. It is not their fault, poor things. They have not the power."

" Then no woman should love or trust them."

" But, to love, it is our nature, we women. To trust is our weakness. But, my little one, we have the revenge with us. We can deceive!"

Alice was horrified at the idea of practising deceit, even towards the man who had deceived her.

" Go, go, little goose! You must think of this. If a man will not be constant— if he tires after a time, it must be that one looks out for a successor to the abdicated."

Alice shuddered.

" Oh, foolish," said her friend, smiling, "see you not that it is you who choose now ? *Autrefois*, it was he who selected you ; now you throw the handkerchief, my Sultana. And who is it that shall be strong enough to resist those azure eyes, that hair of the cloth of gold, and the skin of rubies and cream ? Not I, *ma foi*, if I were a man."

Alice shook her head, and declared that she could never learn this lesson.

But she began to dress with greater care than she had shown for a long time, and she bestowed more pains upon dressing her hair —poor tarnished golden hair !

The keen-eyed Frenchwoman noticed this, and smiled her quiet wicked smile.

" But they are droll, these young girls ! "

And before long Alice noticed that wherever she went she was watched by a tall, dark, handsome youth, whose attention, however, had nothing disrespectful in it.

The old demon of vanity, which had never more than slumbered in her heart since the time when he assisted the other evil passions to work her ruin, awoke, and whispered to her that this was a conquest. Then she began to recall Rosalie's words, and to make excuses to her own conscience. Henry Cormack was deserting her, and she should be left friendless and penniless.

And this man evidently admired her, which Alice thought, with a glance at the glass, was not to be greatly wondered at.

Of course Rosalie was not long in observing Alice's new admirer, and immediately finessed and intrigued on her friend's behalf—not altogether against Alice's wish; and the upshot was that she made the acquaintance of her unknown, who proved to be the son of a nobleman, and very wealthy.

" *Ma foi, Henri mon cher,*" said the Frenchwoman to herself, as she watched the two talking earnestly together, as they sat on a bench in the park, where they had appointed, by letter, to meet, Rosalie going too to play propriety " *ma foi, le bon diable* is going out of his way to relieve you of a bad bargain. You are a favourite with his serene highness, my friend. And now to let you know of this."

That night Rosalie dropped a little note

into the post for Captain Cormack, and the next day he paid her a visit. The two amiable creatures laid their heads together, and devised an excellent plan.

At the next meeting of Alice and her new admirer, Rosalie, in course of conversation, expressed a wish to go to the Crystal Palace the next day to hear a concert that was announced. Alice fell into the snare, and said she should like to go too; and little wonder, for she had led a dull and lonely life for a long time, and had seen little pleasure. The young peer declared nothing would give him greater pleasure than to escort them; so the arrangement was made, and next morning Alice, Rosalie, and he were wandering amid the lovely flowers that deck the Sydenham slopes with all the brilliant hues of the rainbow.

They were just descending one of the terraces, Rosalie hanging a little behind, and Alice leaning on the arm of her companion, and listening to some whispered gallantry, when an exclamation of surprise caused them to look up. It was Captain Cormack.

Alice was ready to sink to the ground. Her companion, who immediately guessed the state of affairs, felt in some doubt about what was likely to follow. Rosalie only looked on with some slight curiosity.

Henry Cormack advanced, smiling. He bowed to Alice's admirer, and shook her by the hand.

"I am exceedingly glad," he said, in a cold, distinct voice, "that you have solved a difficulty which has perplexed me for some time. As you have selected this gentleman for your companion and friend, I can only say I withdraw all claim on your further consideration, and resign readily in his favour. I wish you good-bye."

So saying, he raised his hat, and walked rapidly away.

Of course a scene followed; for though she had ceased to love him, there was one tie—the last hope of a restoration to her good name—which bound Alice to Henry Cormack in spite of indifference and disagreements. Now that was broken, and with it she seemed to lose her hold upon hope. It was another step downward in the deepening darkness.

To do Alice's companion justice, he did not hesitate to do all in his power to make restitution of the advantages which she had sacrificed on his account.

In a few days Alice was mistress of a charming little villa, furnished most luxuriously and expensively. But she could not drown the voice of conscience, or blind her eyes to the knowledge that she had fallen further away from the right, and with but little excuse. Before long the distress of mind she suffered had such an effect upon her nerves that she was laid up with a fever, that compelled her to keep her bed for nearly a month. Even after her recovery she was very weak, and, like most invalids, fretful and impatient. A coolness ensued between her and the young peer, which was never to be removed, for in a short time he was sent abroad on a diplomatic mission, from which he did not return for many years.

Behold Alice then left once more alone, thrown once again into the society of Rosalie for want of companionship, and following her fatal guidance down the gloomy descent whence it is so hard to return.

Every day there dies within her some lingering spark of virtue or goodness. Every day her heart hardens, and her perceptions are blunted. She has become almost a stranger to tears, save when she sheds them on the mock sentiment of a trashy novel or the sham passions of the stage. She has forgotten what it is to blush, and her eyes, with a strange wild light growing in them, are resolutely turned from the past. She has bidden adieu to hope, to remorse, to shame. She has ceased to believe that there is any other love more exalted than a passing passion for a pretty face; and she has grown covetous, for it is only with money that she can purchase the anodyne which makes life bearable.

But when the beauty of the soul is blotted out, it is ordained that outward loveliness shall suffer too. There has come into Alice's face a hardness almost amounting to coarseness; her cheeks are hollow, and the eyes that burn above them burn with unnatural light like the lamps of a charnel-house—for the heart is dead within. And her once so silken-soft hair has lost the glory it had, and as it falls neglected on her shoulders, is dull, and dim, and lustreless.

So her beauty leaves her, for beauty is but an outward revelation of the beauty of the heart.

But we must not watch this sad figure further along its dread path. Let her pass on forlorn amid forlorn revelry, passionless amid a mad semblance of passion and delight—the ghost of a woman once pure, and beautiful, and good, but now lost, desolate, abandoned. And this is man's handiwork! And the world is full of such fair gardens of God that should be—such weed-grown, down-trampled wildernesses that are!

CHAPTER II.

THERE was not much sentiment or ro-
mance, as a rule, in plain, homely Marian
Carlyon. You would not indeed have looked
for any weakness of the sort in that poor,
pale face, whence the bloom and flush of
girlhood had fled for ever. But then there
are periods in the life of all of us—of the
plainest and homeliest—when, like a seemingly sleeping ocean, the heart suddenly
heaves and bursts all barriers; when an
irresistible flood of fierce emotions bursts in
upon us, and, sweeping over us, changes the
whole aspect of our natures for awhile. And
such a heart-heaving and such a resistless
tide of feeling were Marian's after that
momentous meeting in the Mile End Road.

A meeting in the Mile End Road! It does
not sound romantic, does it? If I had called
it an encounter in the Bay of Naples, it would

not have jarred perhaps.   But in this life the most romantic incidents are not always laid in the most appropriate scenery.   What tragedies are enacted in places with such names as Wapping or Hackney, and on what trivial and vulgar things do great events turn! The very crisis of Marian's life was this meeting in the Mile End Road—and to what was it due?   To the drunkenness of the greengrocer's van-driver.   But for the collision with that very commonplace object the Romford 'bus, the van would have rolled on its way rejoicing, and Marian and James would have passed each other within a few yards, and never have known, perhaps, how near they had been. Fate builds up our lives of strange materials, utterly incongruous, and often laughably mean and seemingly unsuitable.

The meeting in the Mile End Road woke the deepest feelings of Marian's nature, and for a time the plain, homely little woman was living in an ideal region of bliss.   All the dark clouds which had so long and apparently so hopelessly closed-in the horizon, had lifted and were scattered, and the golden light of joy and perfect happiness poured in upon her.   Her poor lodging was hung with golden tissue, and all the air was perfume!

The fountain of youth and young hopes was unsealed in her heart, and its waters made pleasant the path of life. The briars and thorns were overgrown and disarmed by the thick blossoms of joy, and comfort, and love which had sprung up as if by a spell at the mere sound of James's voice.

She was once more the Marian Carlyon of old times, only made more beautiful by trial, and suffering, and toil. And so with the girlish tenderness of old days, but not without an inward misgiving that it was romantic and foolish, she wrote to James, and appointed to meet him at that dear old trysting place in the Park where—how long ago!—the barriers that had existed between them had been broken down for the first time, and they stood face to face, and spoke heart to heart — two people ordained by Heaven man and wife.

It was changed, that well-remembered spot!

I suppose the Chief Commissioner of Public Works cannot be expected to know all the shrines and consecrated plots of earth which he ruthlessly overthrows and sweeps away in his pursuit of landscape gardening. But he had gone out of his way, one would suppose, to efface all traces of the quiet nook where James Trefusis had first dared to tell his love to Marian Carlyon. He had come to the conclusion that there were some unaccommodated equestrians in the neighbourhood of Belgravia or Westminster, to whom Rotten Row was either not accessible or not agreeable. So he had devised a most ingenious cantering ground for these individuals which had several advantages. First of all, it was so narrow that two persons could not ride abreast in it; secondly, it was so thickly set with trees that riders were in momentary danger of being swept off their horses; and thirdly, it ended abruptly in a row of spiked railings, and was so narrow just there, that horse and rider alike had every possible chance of impalement, and very little room for turning to escape the peril. Altogether, it would be difficult to conceive a more useful, ornamental, and reasonable way of spending the public money. And it was, and is, so popular among equestrians that, from the day when it was thrown open to the public until this present writing, not even the late lamented Mr. G. P. R. James himself could have seen two horsemen there at a time. But then it makes a capital place for the wheeling of perambulators by nurses, and the wheedling of nurses by the soldiers from the neighbouring barracks.

Of course, as the space for this great work had to be taken from the Park, the walk which had originally run along there was thrown back a little. And in the fresh laying out of the ground consequent on this, the little clump of lilacs was uprooted, and the snug little seat beneath them was removed to quite another part of the Park.

Marian could have found it in her heart to cry when she found the dear old place so completely altered. The change brought before her very forcibly the lapse of time.

It was not possible, thinking as often as she did of Alice, that she should visit the scene of their frequent meetings without calling to mind her sister, and wondering where she could be, and what she could be doing that she never heard or saw anything of her, and that repeated advertisements in the *Times* had failed to elicit any trace of her whereabouts.

She was not aware that a crafty enemy had been working quietly and cunningly to defeat all her efforts to obtain tidings of Alice. Henry Cormack was not the man to

III.   C

be very easily caught tripping in the matter of precautions against the discovery of his roguery and rascality. He had impressed upon Alice the necessity for concealing her name from every one—even from her dear friend Rosalie. Henry Cormack knew that dear friend's character too well to expose her to the temptation of the reward offered by Marian. As for Alice herself, all he had to do was to keep her from seeing the *Times* while her sister was in the habit of advertising in its pages; and in this he found little difficulty, for Alice was as careless and incurious about news as a girl could well be.

Marian was still musing on her sister's disappearance when that mysterious sixth sense, for which psychologists have not yet found a name, told her that James Trefusis was approaching. That sixth sense which belongs to the heart (or brain, which is the same thing) just as sight belongs to the eye, or hearing to the ear, did not deceive her, for in another second or two he was by her side.

" My own ! "

" Dearest James ! "

In those two greetings, simple as they look when written down, there was a meaning which a whole language could hardly find expression for.

He drew her arm within his with the happy unconscious air of a man who is claiming nothing more than is his own right. And then he led her away to a retired seat, neither speaking a word, because their hearts, too full for utterance, were communing in silence.

Then James began his story from the beginning, and told Marian how he had succeeded in selling his patent, and how prosperous and wealthy he had become. All this Marian knew well, but she did not interrupt him. She had hungered so very very long in her weary self-seclusion for the sound of that voice, that it seemed now as if she could listen to it for ever.

" All my good fortune and prosperity, Marian, could have no charm for me. I was sick and weary of the world—sick of the fortune which kept aloof when I most needed it, and showered down upon me when I had no longer any desire for it. I wanted to creep away somewhere and go to sleep, to wake up some day in Heaven, and find you. But they would not let me rest; and I felt that it was better to struggle on a bit, in the hopes of our meeting again by chance—as we

have done.   If it had not been for that hope,
I should not have cared to go on working.   I
should have flung all the money and fame
to the winds, and shut my door against the
world, and all its interests and troubles, long
ago ! "

" Then you always hoped to meet me
again ?   I did not think you would have
known me, for I am greatly altered,
James."

" I could have sworn to those dear
gray eyes of yours anywhere, my Marian.
Altered !   Do you suppose, when a man
really and truly loves a woman, he does not
know the changes that time will work.
True love is not blind——"

" Oh, yes it is, James, for I know your's
is true, and yet you cannot see what a poor,
disfigured creature I am.   Honestly now,
James !—have I not got very plain indeed ? "

She laid her hand on his arm, and looked
into his face with her eager gray eyes, trying
to read his answer before he spoke.   And
she did read it, for a smile of infinite
happiness sweetened the tender expression
of her mouth before he had answered a
word.

" My Marian," he said ; " still my

Marian. Not altered the tiniest wee bit in the world to me! But how anxious you are about your looks, puss. Have you grown vain?"

She shook her head gravely.

"It is not on account of my poor plain face that I am so distressed, James. But you are so determined to make me your wife, whether I will or no"—she smiled tenderly as she said this—"that I am anxious for your sake. What should I do if some day they were to say to you, 'How could you ever think of marrying a woman so disfigured as that?' It would break my heart to think you were ever so little ashamed of me."

"I should be utterly unworthy of you, my own one, if I could be that for an instant. Besides, do not I know your value, treasure of mine?—beauty that cannot fade, the beauty of the heart and the mind. Your face is dearer to me and fairer than the loveliest creation artist ever dreamed of."

"I cannot doubt you, James. I could not love you as I do if I doubted your lightest word; so I must believe this, and the belief is of infinite comfort to me. Ah, you do not know what it cost me to tear

myself away from you when first the consciousness of this affliction came upon me."

" You did not believe me, then ! "

" I did not, even then, know what it is to
love truly—much as I loved you. I have
learnt to love since then, dearest, with a love
that has grown and strengthened in absence,
and despair, and separation."

There was no foolish hesitation in this
woman's words, when she thus laid open the
secrets of her heart. Why should there be ?
The perfect equality of the highest and
purest passion that can exist between man
and woman is due to the communion of soul
with soul—of essences too lofty to be
influenced by the weakness of this world, or
considerations of the relation of the sexes.
Marian felt that there was nothing to blush
at or conceal in the noble love she bore to
this man. She had been prepared, when she
thought by so acting she was doing him the
best service, to part from him and bear away
into solitude the love which was more than
half her life, there to nurse it with sad
memories and irremediable sorrow. And if
she could do this, why should she not
bestow it upon him, now that she might do
so without reserve or false modesty ? It

enhanced a gift, which real modesty made
her consider a poor one, to tell all its virtues
and the price which it had cost her. Any
man who has ever been blessed with that
most precious of all Heaven's gifts, the
great and abiding affection of a true woman,
will know that she never seemed so truly a
woman as when she looked him straight in
the eyes and said, clearly and deliberately,
"I love you!" And he will also understand why James Trefusis sighed a great
sigh of relief and happiness when Marian
spoke of the deep love she bore him, without
a blush and without a change of tone, as if
it were as natural a part of her being as that
she breathed and moved.

"My poor child," he said, stroking the
hand she had placed in his, "you must have
suffered indeed. And what weary work
yours must have been."

"No, James! I won't be ungrateful to
my work. Work was my companion and
comforter. But for it I must have sunk
indeed into listlessness and despair. But I
toiled on, for work's sake—hardly because I
hoped."

"And I, too, worked on—but I worked
to win, Marian. I was desponding at times,

and almost ready to relinquish the thought of our meeting again, but I determined to work for your sake—even though we never might meet, but because I could say to myself, 'I am working that I may win the woman I love.' But it was very dark at times, darling—only the remembered light in those dear eyes lighted me to my toil."

In this way these two people talked over their trials and toils, in the enjoyment of their triumph. For it seemed to them that they had suffered to the full now, and were to take the reward of their labour and of their patience. Are they fated to enjoy it yet?

By-and-by Marian, having told the long story of her suffering and the struggle she had had ere she was fortunate enough to be appointed the mistress of St. Pacifica's schools, spoke of Alice, and told James of her mysterious disappearance.

James was more alarmed than he cared to show, for he remembered the communication Alice had made to him. He asked Marian if she had heard of her sister's attachment to Lord Lacquoigne's son. Marian shook her head mournfully, and said, "Yes; it was that which led to her being discharged from her ladyship's service."

" Did she suppose that this Captain Vorian," James asked, with a bitter emphasis on the title, " had anything to do with Alice's subsequent disappearance ? "

Marian could not tell, but she believed not. Captain Vorian had since married the eldest daughter of Mr. Orr, her old employer.

" That old scoundrel's daughter ! I hope she is only half as bad as her father, and then perhaps poor Alice will be in some degree revenged for the cruelty she suffered at Lady Lacquoigne's hands. Did I ever tell you of my interview with Orr at his office in the City ? I never was nearer a breach of the peace in my life than I was then. But I believe the old villain will suffer for it yet. He cannot go on much longer—the golden idol has feet of clay, and fall he must before many years are over, and then won't I rejoice ! "

" James, James ! I'm afraid you have grown sadly revengeful."

" By heaven, a man does not suffer or see others suffer, as I have done, without recording a few vows of vengeance; and I have several. There is your father's murderer, Henry Cormack—the man of whom I am to purchase the foundry, by-the-bye, at the end of this year—I have a bitter score to settle with him, though I own it is difficult to see any way to an excuse for bringing him to an account. Then there is old Orr; and I suppose—I fear—there is also this Captain Vorian. With all and each, if I can only see my opportunity, I have a heavy reckoning to make; and as sure as I live and breathe, when that time comes, they shall have cause to remember me!"

"Oh, James, it terrifies me to hear you speak in that way. We should forgive our enemies——"

"So I will—when I have done with them! There are some wrongs inflicted on those we love—inflicted in the most heartless and agonising forms—which drive all the forgiveness out of a man and harden his heart. And these are such wrongs, that I can't and won't forgive them!"

Marian saw it was useless to argue with him now, for the memory of these men's misdeeds was rousing all the anger in his nature.

Did he really mean all these vindictive threats ?

Well, I incline to believe not. But the best men are carried away sometimes by their scorn and anger at wickedness which they cannot understand the pleasure or motive of. To James Trefusis, Henry Cormack and Mr. Orr, instead of seeming men whose callous hearts and unrestrained passions blunted their perceptions of right and wrong, appeared to be fiends who delighted in iniquity for its own sake. So just in the degree that he was himself in reality generous and earnest, he raged against these demons, until, without knowing it, he was nourishing designs quite as unchristian and improper as theirs.

Marian turned the conversation to other subjects, and James's thirst for revenge died out. They talked of the future, and it was agreed that as soon as Cormack resigned possession of the foundry and Polvrehan, they were to marry, and go down to settle in their native valley. How bright the future looked !

In the meantime Marian resigned her appointment at the school of St. Pacifica's. But as there was some time yet to elapse before James would get possession of Polvrehan, and as there was some difficulty in finding a successor, she consented, at the special request of the Rev. Mr. Rudgeworth, to continue to manage the schools until they could meet with a suitable teacher.

James was a little opposed to this at first; but Marian declared she was sorry to part with her little folk, and should like to stay with them as long as she could. She further pointed out that by so doing she would be making some return for the kindness with which she had been treated.

" But you must be very weary of teaching, Marian."

" Nay, I am used to it now, James; and, besides, I shall hardly feel that I deserve to win if I do not work as long as I am needed."

So James consented, and Marian promised Mr. Rudgeworth to stay; and it was agreed that her leaving should not be mentioned to the children until the day of her departure came, because she was a favourite with her pupils, and they would perhaps become unsettled and troublesome when they heard she was going.

CHAPTER III.

"COULD IT HAVE BEEN A GHOST?"

THE Honourable Henry Vorian is lounging over his breakfast in solitary gran-
deur, the Honourable Mrs. Vorian having
elected to take that meal in her bedroom.
The Honourable Henry is not particularly
distressed to hear it, and discusses his
lonely repast with a cheerful appetite. He
has just taken up the paper and turned his
chair round to the fire, when a knock comes
at the door.

"Come in."

A footman enters.

"M' lord, sir—m' lord wishes to speak
with you, sir, if you are disengaged."

"Ask him up."

The flunkey disappears, and the Honourable Henry Vorian begins to muse on his
parent's visit.

"My father, eh? I wonder what the deuce he wants? Not money again, I hope "—you see his lordship has been bleeding his son just as her ladyship has been drawing on Honoria—"Not money again, I hope. He can't have it, if it is, for I'm cleaned out, and her ladyship up-stairs is not in an amiable mood, so I can't get anything out of her. Besides, hang it all, I didn't marry to support my father and mother!"

By the time this thought has occurred to this very dutiful and affectionate son, Lord Lacquoigne is ushered in.

His son does not rise to greet him; but there had never been more ceremony than affection between them, so his lordship takes a seat on the opposite side of the fire.

"You're late this morning, Henry."

"Oh, no; about the usual time."

"I suppose you're in training for Parlia-mentary duties, eh? They do keep you up doosid late in the Commons."

"Oh, I've given up all notion of that. Scrooby said it would cost about a thousand pounds, there's such a confounded lot of freemen in the place, and tin is rather scarce with us just now, so I told him not to bother any more about it."

"I am sorry for that, because just now the Government has such a narrow majority that they are ready to do almost any thing for a vote, and Arthur is old enough now. I dare say it might be done cheaper. You'll reconsider it, won't you?"

"No. I've decided; and there's an end of it."

"I'm very sorry to hear it. You had a splendid career before you, and it would have fitted you for your duties in the Upper House."

"Very likely. But may I ask if I am indebted for this visit to your desire to see me in Parliament?"

"No, Henry—I have come on a rather delicate matter."

(" Confound it," thought the young man; "he does want some money, that's clear.")

"What may it be, my lord?"

"I really hardly know how to begin. But it is due to our name and family that I should not hesitate—to——In short—well, you see, I—I don't think you can be quite aware, Henry, of the talk which is occasioned by Honoria's going about so much with Cantlow. He's a designing scoundrel, that fellow—a low blackguard! You should hear what is said of him at Noodle's. I was standing in the bay-window with old Major-General Tampion the other day, when Cantlow rode by in the phaeton with Honoria, and the old gentleman spoke of him in the most severe terms, and said he thought you could hardly be aware of the sort of man he is, or you would forbid him your house. Gad, sir ! all town's in a buzz about him and your wife."

" Let town buzz," said Henry angrily ; "I don't care a straw for that. If I've confidence in Honoria's good sense, that's quite enough. We have rows in plenty as it is, and I don't want to have any additional ones just because a lot of scandal-mongering dowagers set their venomous old tongues wagging—I hope they may wither! Besides, the beggar saves me a good deal of trouble, for I hate lugging women about to shows and fêtes and all such infernal foolery."

" You have not the spirit or the feelings of a Vorian, sir, or you wouldn't suffer it."

" By Jove, I'm rather sick of feeling like

III. D

a Vorian, my lord. I wish I were somebody else."

"So do I, most heartily, sir."

"Thank you!"

"At any rate, if you don't respect the
family name, you should regard your own
character."

"Oh, I'll look after that!"

"Well, if you do, I think you'll find that
you have the character of being a fool who
is blind to his own dishonour. You're a
laughing-stock, sir, egad,—a regular laughing-stock at all the clubs."

"Curse 'em! I'll teach them to laugh!"
exclaimed Henry, goaded to anger by his
father's taunts.

"I'm afraid you won't frighten any of
them, because you have got the reputation
of being afraid of Cantlow."

"The devil I have! Then it's time I
took some steps to prove the contrary."

Lord Lacquoigne having thus succeeded
in awakening his son to a sense of the
family dignity, took his departure before
very long.

"Where's your mistress?" asked Henry
Vorian of the footman who came to clear
the breakfast table.

" I'll inquire, sir," said that domestic.

Henry presently learnt that the Honourable Mrs. Vorian was in her boudoir, whereupon he sent up word to say he was desirous of speaking with her if she were not engaged. On receiving a request to step up to the boudoir, he obeyed, not without an uncomfortable feeling—the fore-knowledge of a very unpleasant storm coming.

" What are your desires ? " asks the lady languidly as he enters the room.

" My desire," her husband answers brusquely, opening the campaign at once, " my desire is that that confounded puppy Cantlow shall not come here in the way he does."

" Pardon me, but he is not a visitor of yours, and does not in any way interfere with you. My desire is that he shall come."

" And I forbid it ! By Jove, madam, I shall have to believe the scandals which are afloat about you if you persist in this conduct."

" Henry Vorian, you are a fool—and what is more, a vulgar fool. How dare you insult me in that way ? "

" You shouldn't provoke me ! "

" I do not."

" You do. You refuse to obey my directions !"

" At the risk of provoking you ever so
much, I intend to do that."

" Have a care, madam ! "

" Of what, may I ask ? "

" Of bringing that adventurer into this
house. By Jove, I'll kick him out."

" I think not."

" Egad, madam, he *shan't* come ! "

" Sir, Major Cantlow is an honourable
gentleman, who takes pity upon the wife
whom you neglect and insult. If you dare
to be guilty of the slightest rudeness to
him, you shall suffer for it. I will quit this
roof and return to my father."

" I wish to heaven you would."

" The matter will not end there, sir, for
you may rely on my father's exposing your
treatment of me. The law shall liberate me
from ties which you disregard; and the
grounds on which I shall demand my release shall be made public, to your disgrace,
sir ! "

" Come, will you give up this man's
acquaintance ? "

" No, I will not ! It would be a base

and cowardly return for the honourable and disinterested kindness he has shown me!"

"I'll call the beggar out and shoot him."

"That is mere idle bluster. People don't duel in these days; and if you did, you would probably find him the better shot."

"Come, Honoria, let us argue this calmly! My father has been here to speak of the rumours which are circulated about you and this fellow. Now I have every confidence in your good sense, but really——"

"But really I decline to condescend to any argument on the matter!"

"You impracticable devil!" muttered the honourable gentleman to himself.

He was quite at a loss what to do. He had not expected open rebellion and defiance.

"Now, sir, having, I presume, indulged in enough insult and brutality towards me, you will not object to leave me."

"I shall order the servants to refuse this scoundrel admittance."

"If by that abusive word—which you would not dare use in his presence—you intend Major Cantlow, you can spare yourself the trouble. He has left town for a couple of days. During that interval you will have time to reflect before you take a step which, I warn you most distinctly, will lead to much that will be most painful and embarrassing."

Henry Vorian gave an impatient "Pish!" and strode up and down the room.

"I think we had better come to that understanding. It will give you two days to decide what course you intend to pursue. You must let me put my position clearly before you. I consented to marry you for the position and independence of a married woman——"

"And a title!"

"My father was wealthy enough to buy your beggarly title three times over, so that insult falls harmless. I repeat, I married you because I was tired of being kept in restraint, and led about like an animal for sale, and because I wanted the independent position of a married woman. Considering what I paid for that freedom, by marrying a man of your tastes and disposition, I am not in the least inclined to let go a hair's breadth of my privilege. I care no more for Major Cantlow than I do for you, and could give up either to-morrow without a murmur; but it is the principle that I uphold, and will uphold. I am mistress of my own actions, and will not be dictated to in the smallest degree. There! now you have my case. You had better go to that precious father of yours, and lay it before him, and take his advice. Until then, good morning!"

She made him a stately bow, which he returned, and then left the room.

Now there were two things which Honoria said during this conversation which were not exactly true.

She said, in the first place, that Major Cantlow had left town for two days. Whereas she was quite well aware that he had promised to come that very afternoon and convoy her to the Botanical Gardens.

She said, in the second place, that she cared no more for Major Cantlow than she did for her husband. Whereas, while she hated the latter, she really entertained for the former a passion which he had carefully fanned by constant attentions and fed with delicate compliments.

On the whole, then, we may, I think, set down that grand declaration of her intentions and wishes in marrying to a desire to conceal her real object in thus obstinately

declining to discontinue her acquaintance
with the Major.

Henry Vorian left his house in no very
enviable frame of mind. A man who has
open rebellion and flat defiance staring him
in the face at home, is under any circumstances not pleasantly situated ; but when
the reason of the revolt is one that so nearly
touches his honour, the awkwardness of his
position is infinitely increased. He was not
so persuaded of his wife's sincerity in that
last matrimonial declaration of hers as to
overlook the fact that her refusal to give up
her friendship with the Major was capable
of a very disastrous construction. He could
not close his eyes to that.

What was he to do ? Perhaps, after all,
the counsel she had given was the best.
He would go and ask his father's advice
on the matter.

Lord Lacquoigne was utterly at a loss.
The outburst on the part of the hitherto
easy-going Honoria was more than startling
—it was ominous. The aristocratic nose
having been called into the consultation,
failed to hit off the right scent ; but, nevertheless, the wisest suggestion thrown out in
conclave was her ladyship's, who proposed

that his lordship and Henry should go to Mr. Orr the next day.

Henry Vorian did not care to go home under existing circumstances, so he spent the rest of the day at the mansion in May-fair. It was not a cheerful day. His father, and mother, and himself, as they dined off scrag of mutton, served up on silver dishes by several footmen, felt that it was anything but a dinner of herbs with content—though the cook had tried to palm off the mutton as lamb by sending up mint sauce with it.

These three guilty people looked at one another, and felt that the just punishment of their own wrong-doing was coming upon them. They had turned a solemn service, which should link hearts together, into a mere formula of the money market—they had bid Mammon chain together those whom God had not joined, and they were reaping the reward of their iniquity.

Late in the evening, Henry Vorian bid his noble parents good night, lit his cigar, and sauntered off homewards.

It was a sultry autumn night, not altogether fine, for there were heavy banks of cloud resting on the horizon, and scat-

tered troops of rainy-looking vapours occasionally scudded across the sky, obscuring a
pallid and watery moon. It was a night
quite in keeping with Henry Vorian's
state of mind, and he walked slowly along
Piccadilly, just keeping his cigar alight
rather than really smoking, and watching
with half-attentive eyes the crowds that
passed him. The crowds were the ordinary London crowds, but with one or
two characteristic ingredients belonging to
Piccadilly. There were swells in evening
costume going to or returning from balls,
dinners, or evening parties; and there were
gaily-dressed women, with impudent smiles,
and cheeks whose roses were raddle; and
there were the sleepy drivers of huge carts of
vegetables on their way to Covent Garden.

At the corner of a street, Henry
Vorian's attention was attracted to an
itinerant coffee stall, whereat a cabman,
a crossing-sweeper, and one or two other
night-birds, male and female, were standing. A flaring naphtha lamp lit up the
group, and shed a glow on the faces of
passers-by. There was an odd Rem-
brandtish effect about the scene, and he
stopped for a moment to look at it.

As he turned from it to continue his walk homeward, a shrill, unnatural laugh, just behind him, made him look back. He saw two women entering the circle of light. The yellow, smoky glare fell on their faces.

The one nearest him was pale and thin. Her yellow hair, heavy with the moisture of night, was carelessly looped up, as if it had fallen from the comb. Her blue eyes were sunken, and had a cold, hard stare. Her cheeks were hollow, and the shrill laugh—it was her's—that had attracted Henry Vorian's attention, ended in a sharp husky cough that seemed to pierce her like a knife.

Henry Vorian started, as well he might, for a spectre of the past stood before him. He uttered an involuntary exclamation. The woman looked up and saw him—and then, after one short glance, turned, with a strange plaintive cry, and fled. As soon as he could recover his presence of mind, he followed her; but there were carts and cabs passing at the time, and carriages from Lady Palmerston's assembly, and the streets were crowded, and he failed to catch sight of her again.

"Great Heaven, could it have been a ghost?" he murmured, as he once more turned his face homeward.

Alas! Henry Vorian, not the ghost of a dead woman—would it were! It is the ghost of departed beauty and innocence—of a living woman!

CHAPTER IV.

THE MAJOR FOR ONCE RELUCTANT TO DO A WRONG.

"TO what is all this bringing us?"

"To what, indeed?"

The first speaker is the Honourable Honoria Vorian; the second Major Cantlow.

The Honourable Henry Vorian had not long quitted his mansion, when, on the principle of the Dutch weather-glass, Major Cantlow entered it. Honoria, with some slight perturbation and not a few eruptive-looking blushes, told him all that had taken place between her and her husband—or rather as much of it as put her in the position of a woman who was undergoing misery and suspicion on his (Major Cantlow's) account.

The Major pensively fondled one dyed whisker, and wondered what was to come of this. Honoria, who knew less of the world, propounded that question at once.

She fully expected—from her experience of men who loved other people's wives, an experience founded on the perusal of ordinary novels—that the Major would open his arms, and invite her to fall upon his noble though padded bosom, in the touching words, "Whatever comes, you have at least a refuge here!"

But the Major was not such an ass.

A man who lives, if not exactly on his wits, at all events of his neighbour's want of the article, is not in the habit of committing himself rashly to any step. The Major was such a man, and he did not make any attempt to invite Honoria to repose upon his chest until he had calculated how far such a step would resemble the killing of the goose to which he was indebted for golden eggs—an act of ansericide that he had not the remotest intention of being guilty of.

A rapid review of the facts of the case reminded him of one thing—that Mrs. Vorian owed her wealth, not to her husband, but her father. It remained to be proved whether the latter would still continue his generous allowance to her if she quitted the husband he had selected for her. Thoroughly impressed with this conviction, the Major did not open his arms and offer Honoria a refuge from cruelty and neglect within their amiable shelter. He took her hand respectfully, dropped his voice to the lowest note in its compass, and said with great solemnity,—

" Did I merely consult the selfish dictates of my heart—the hopes and dreams of which, Honoria, cannot have been quite concealed from you—I would bid you seek beneath my humble roof the devotion and regard which you do not find here. I would ask you—may I say it ?—to spurn and bid defiance to the hypocrital horror of a short-sighted world in the deep and unbounded love which I can no longer conceal that I bear for you, Honoria! But I must not be selfish. I must prove my affection for you by refusing to make myself unutterably happy at the cost of suffering to you. I am a poor man—a penniless—a worse than penniless one. I should but offer you a share of penury and wretchedness. It must not be."

" Oh, Alfred, you forget that I am rich !"

"Well, you see," said the Major, dropping unguardedly into a business-like tone in his deep interest about the matter, "your allowance depends entirely on your father, and he might withdraw that any day, and would, most likely, when he had heard that we had run—had determined to unite our fortunes for good and evil despite the malice and envy of a cold and heartless world!" Here, you will observe, the Major rose to his subject again.

"My father is too much attached to me to allow me to suffer because I follow the dictates of my heart."

"If you could be quite sure of that, why you know I don't see the slightest obstacle in the world."

"At all events, I can apply to him at once for such a sum of money as shall secure us against want for some time to come."

"Ah, yes. But you may as well make it something handsome. What is the limit now that you think you might go to ?"

And then the Major began to discuss with Honoria the exact amount at which it would be worth his while to run away with her.

You must not suppose that Honoria even was so blind as not to see how mercenary the Major was. She had been born and brought up in a family where one of the earliest notions instilled into the young mind was that whatever people do for you is done for money. She detected the Major's baseness at once. It was a severe blow to her, for hitherto she had been under the foolish impression that he really loved her. But it was too late to withdraw now. She had admitted her regard for him, and had in fact almost proposed their elopement in so many words. Then again she could not be more unhappy with this man than she was with her husband, and in flying with him she would at least bring shame and misery upon one who had wedded her without love and neglected her without pity.

But I am bound to allow that Honoria made her unholy contract with Major Cantlow with her eyes open.

You wonder, perhaps. But revenge is a stronger passion than love, and women especially, I fear, will make any sacrifices at its shrine. If you doubt the statement, look around you and note what is passing.

III.   E

What happened a little while ago? Why, the University of Oxford, which, I take it, is the very personification and embodiment of the middle-aged feminine mind, proved the truth of what I say, and rejected a man who was essentially the representative of scholarship and all that graces the University,—and all for a passing political squabble. As if Alma Mater had any more to do with politics than Mater Familias! But A. M. lost her temper, and accordingly lost a representative who did her honour.

Honoria Vorian was stung to the heart by the discovery of Cantlow's baseness. But the discovery did not drive her from the step she meditated. She either hoped to waken his better feelings, or she intended to make one act help her to vengeance against both her husband and him.

She was too shrewd to let the Major see that she noticed the very business-like spirit in which he bargained with her. She discussed the question from the same point of view quite calmly. It was quite possible, she thought, to get a very handsome advance from papa, and to prevail on him to forgive them before it was quite exhausted.

" I will write to papa at once, and press my request very urgently; and I feel sure there is no difficulty. What had you better do ? "

The Major suggested that he should take the letter to papa.

" Oh, there's no necessity for that; it might look suspicious, I am afraid."

" Ah," thought the Major, " she thinks I should sack the money and never come near her again ; " but what he said was, " I see every necessity for haste. It is hardly possible that your husband, when he returns, should fail to hear I have been here—and have stayed a considerable time," —he glanced at the little ormulu clock on the mantelpiece. A fat, fatuous little Cupid on the top was engaged in singeing a gilded butterfly with a torch. " The result would be disastrous. By going to Mr. Orr myself, I might hasten matters."

" You have other arrangements to make."

" Oh, we can get a cab to the station, and be over in France before our absence is discovered." And he thought to himself, it would be a pity to engage the cab unless they were quite sure of the money.

" Marland, my maid, is accustomed to

go to papa on similar errands. She will take a cab and go, and be back in an hour. In the meantime I will take advantage of her absence to pack a few things in my trunk, and you can make your preparations. Be at the end of the street with a cab in time to get to the station. Till then farewell."

She held out her face for him to kiss; and so they parted.

"Whew!" whistled the Major as soon as he was in the open air; "Here's a pretty go! Whew! It makes me as hot as if I had been marching under a tropical sun. She took me quite by surprise. I did not mean it to go as far as this—by Jove, I didn't. Canty, my boy—Canty, my boy! you've been and gone and put your foot into it considerably! You have lived to your age, and have had the good sense never to take a wife of your own, and now I'm cursed if you're not going to take some-one else's! Egad, it only shows what one may be let into without the least intention. Figure in the Divorce Court, eh? Well, what matter? Lots of fine fellows and elegant gentlemen have done the same— and haven't got the money you'll get. Of course there'll be damages; but old Orr must pay them. Still I must confess I should prefer this sort of thing "—and the Major brought up his arm as if he held a pistol, and took aim at a lamp-post, closing one little bloodshot eye very deliberately in order to do so accurately.

"It'll be a doose of a thing, though! And she'll be such a confounded tie until she gets broken-in; but then you see, Canty, you don't often get money without some incumbrance. After all, this is only a woman, and you have been hampered with —and got rid of—many a one before this."

So with a gay ghost of a whistle the Major struts away to his lodgings, where he packs up his goods and chattels—no very great store—in his portmanteau, pays his landlady, and then goes to call on a few friends, from whom he borrows, whenever he can, small sums of money, in case of disappointment in the papa quarter. For he feels now he has risked all, and must in honour—honour, forsooth!—keep his promise to Honoria, whatever occurs.

The faithful Marland speeds off to Mr. Orr's offices in the City. She is at first refused admittance; Mr. Orr is so very busy.

But the letter she carries procures her an entrance into the millionaire's sanctum, where she finds him looking very haggard and ill. He motions Marland to a chair, and takes Honoria's letter over to his desk, where he sits down to read it.

It evidently requires a great mental effort on his part to concentrate his attention on the paper before him. His mind evidently wanders away after he has got through a line or so, and he has to recall it, which he does painfully and with great difficulty.

Marland hears him murmur, "Poor girl! poor girl! What will she do?" and she at once concludes that her mistress has been writing about her domestic unhappiness. But even Marland's conclusions are not invariably sound.

At last, after many fits of abstraction, Mr. Orr succeeds in coming to the end of his daughter's communication. Then he sits for a minute or so with his head resting on his hands, musing. Finally, he rings the bell, and gives some whispered directions to his cashier, who answers the summons. That functionary bows and disappears, and returns about a quarter

of an hour aferwards with a small bag of
sovereigns and a pile of bank-notes. These
Mr. Orr secures in a large envelope, and
gives Marland, with a brief note addressed
to the Honourable Mrs. Vorian, which he
has scribbled off hastily while the cashier
was absent.

"Good gracious!" says Honoria, when
Marland returns from her errand; "how
generous!"

Mr. Orr has sent her about four times
the amount of money that she asked for.
But when she reads his note she does not
seem quite so delighted, and looks puzzled
and bewildered.

It is hardly worth while mentioning,
except as an instance of the way in which
all the movements and relations of great
people are known to the world; but when
Marland left Mr. Orr's office, a short,
commonplace-looking man, who had been
lounging against a post opposite the entrance, crossed over, and addressed himself
very familiarly to a tall, dark, shabby-
genteel individual, who seemed to be waiting about on the look-out for a job.

"Who's that?" asks the short man.

"Oh, her? Why she's his daughter's

slavey. The chief ain't been‾ or sent, has he ? "

" Not to me. But I s'pose he will before long."

" All right."

This conversation, which has been carried on with an air of great carelessness and unconcern, having been brought to a conclusion, the two separate and resume their places and their indifferent bearing.

Marland finds that in her absence the Honourable Mrs. Vorian has been packing up a large trunk. On inquiry, she learns from her mistress that they are about to make a short stay at Brighton, but that the plan has been decided on at very short notice; and as Marland was out, her mistress had to make all the preparations herself.

When she learns that her master has not been home, and that no letters are come, Marland is, I dare say, a ·little puzzled to think how her mistress can be aware of this very sudden arrangement, but she does not trouble herself enough about it to mention her wonder to any one.

The evening comes on.

In the quiet dusk of the hour, between

sunset and moonrise, Honoria going upstairs for some trifle which she has, it
appears, omitted to pack up, passes her
child's door. She pauses and listens. She
can hear the boy's regular breathing, which
tells he is sound asleep. So she opens the
door very, very quietly, and steals in to
look at him. She bends over his pink,
sleepy face, and leaves a kiss on his cheek,
and I hope and believe a tear on his brow,
for something twinkles there, until the
child, half-roused from his sleep, puts up
his hand scarcely consciously, and wipes it
away.

Then Honoria goes downstairs, and
putting her bonnet and cloak in readiness
on the table, sits at the window, watching.
She is in a burning fever of terror and
impatience. At any moment, she fears her
husband may return, and then her plans
will be defeated. Or the Major may delay
his coming until it is too late to catch the
train. She gazes out into the gathering
gloom, with fiercely impatient eyes.

She orders the footman to carry her large
box down into the little breakfast-room
opening on the hall. It will be more
expeditiously removed to the cab from

there. She puts on her things, though they feel so warm that she is nearly stifled. But what does that matter? She will be ready to get into the cab at once. She tries to allay her impatient restlessness by devising these little artifices for speed. And every minute she looks out of the window, and gazes up the street eagerly.

At last a cab stops at the corner. But at the same moment some one turns that corner and walks down the street. Her heart stops almost, for she is nearly sure it is her husband. But she is deceived. He passes by, and her soul is relieved. Then she looks towards the cab, and sees the Major standing beside it, making signs of haste.

She hurries down to the door. The footman is standing there, looking out of the narrow strip of window at the side.

" Charles, here's half a sovereign. Just carry my box to the cab that is waiting at the corner."

Charles looks astonished at first. Then a light seems to dawn upon him—he reflects ; but the next instant says, " Yes, m'm," and carries out the trunk with great alacrity. He places it on the roof of the cab, and takes the opportunity of looking very hard at the Major, who has screwed himself into as small a compass as possible in the darkest corner.

He loiters a minute, apparently from politeness, as his mistress is entering the cab, and he hears the Major mention the railway station to which he wishes to be driven, to the cabman, who has got down to shut the door.

" Drive like —— " the rest is lost in the slam of the cab door; and no great loss either, I fear !

Some hours afterwards Captain Vorian comes home, and Charles, suppressing the mention of the half-sovereign, relates what has taken place.

His master is utterly aghast. He staggers as if the news were a great sledge-hammer blow on the forehead.

" Gone ! Gone ! " is all that he can gasp out. Presently he recovers himself a little.

" You're sure it was Major Cantlow ? "

" Oh, yes, sir, certain. I looked in at the cab window, which he'd stopped it at the corner out of the light of the gas-lamp."

" You saw his face ? "

"Oh, quite plain, sir, through the front window."

"And what the devil were you doing there?"

"I carried out the box, sir, please. My mistress ordered me to do it."

"And you did it?"

"Yes, sir."

Thereupon Henry Vorian gives a straight hit from the shoulder which alights just between Charles's eyes, and knocks him flat on the mat. And then the Honourable Henry Vorian turns, and leaves the deserted house, slamming the great door behind him violently. He hurries away towards town again, and hailing the first Hansom that came along the road with its single lamp glaring like a Cyclops, orders the driver to take him to Mayfair. Arrived there, he hastens to his father's house, and clamours at the door, until he is admitted by a drowsy footman, who has been sitting up to smoke a furtive pipe in the kitchen, with his head up the chimney. As soon as he obtains an entrance, Henry, without ceremony, rushes upstairs to his father and mother's room.

"May I come in!" he asks, opening the door at the same time.

"Eh, what!" asks my lord, awakened out of his first doze, while the aristocratic nose peers out, inquiringly, from a night-cap frill.

"She's gone, sir! by Heaven, she's gone!"

"Who—where?" still asks my lord, not thoroughly conscious.

"Who? Why my wife, and with that infernal scoundrel, Cantlow!"

CHAPTER V.

HAMPTON RACES.

"WHY, James, what has put you out?" asks Marian, as she greets her affianced husband in the Park, where they have arranged to meet, it being Wednesday afternoon, and a half-holiday for "Teacher."

"Enough to put any one out, darling. That fellow, Cormack, has written to my lawyer to say that circumstances over which he has no control will oblige him to put off his surrender of the estate for several months."

"But can he?"

"Just what I asked my lawyer, and he said he could. For it seems, in my anxiety to get hold of dear old Polvrehan, I closed the bargain too rapidly, and did not secure my own interests sufficiently."

"What a pity! But he may go on like this for ever—what is to prevent him?"

"Well, in the first place, he won't get his money until he delivers up possession; and in the next I can cry off, if I choose."

"You won't do that, I know; I should be very sorry if you did. So we must wait patiently. We have waited, haven't we dear?"

"Yes, far too long. But we will not let this fellow mar our happiness, though he puts out our plans a little."

"What can we do?"

"Charlie Crawhall, an old friend of mine, an artist, tells me that he has seen a lovely little place to let at Hampton. It would be just the very place for us, and we could stay there and be so happy until we got possession of Polvrehan."

"Dear old Polvrehan! Well, I suppose we shall get it some day."

"To be sure. But in the meantime we can make a very happy home of our riverside villa at Hampton."

"Have you seen it?"

"No, but Crawhall is going down there to-morrow, and he has promised me a seat in his trap. If I like the place, I can take it at once—and then——"

"And then, James?" says Marian, archly.

"Then I shall make the dearest little woman in the world my wife—and 'so they married and lived happy ever afterwards,' as the old fairy tales say."

Before James and Marian parted that night, they had fixed their wedding-day, and spoke of their married life as a certainty. Is anything certain in this world?

When the evening begins to grow dark, they turn their steps towards Duke Street, St. James's, where Marian's old friend, Mrs. Bartlett, resides now, having at last attained to the height of her ambition.

Marian had met her accidentally in the street, and learning her address went to see her. Of course she was not long with the kind-hearted little soul before she had made a full confession of her attachment for James, and of her approaching marriage.

Mrs. Bartlett, good, motherly woman, took an immense and lively interest in the engagement at once—as all good, motherly women would do. She was delighted to learn that there was a difficulty about the lovers meeting, as Marian, of course, could not ask James to her lodgings, or visit him at his chambers.

"There I declare! And if I'm not the luckiest Bartlett in the world to have no one in my parlours, where I sit myself now, so you can come to see me as often as ever you like—the pair of you, and dine and take your teas, and make it your home, and me your mother, my dear, which I do feel like to you—and why not? For though a boy, I have had a child of my own, and you seem to fill a place that ought to be filled in an old woman's heart, my dear." Whereupon she kisses Marian, with her eyes twinkling with tears.

Marian, you may be sure, is very grateful to the kind little body for her thoughtfulness and affection; and when she and James meet, they generally finish the evening after their walk in the Park by taking tea with Mrs. Bartlett.

On this evening that merry, good-tempered woman is more than ordinarily cheerful, when she hears of James's proposal to go and take a house at Hampton, and marry at once.

"Lor, it's so lovely and romantic there, where I have often gone with poor B., when living, for a holiday, and saw the pictures, and the Park, which is beautiful. Why,

III. F

there, I declare if I won't run down and see you sometimes; that is, if so be you make this house in Duke Street your home, my dears, when you come to town, which will, I hope, be often."

They assured her they should only be too happy to call and see her whenever they came to town. But it was getting late now, and they made preparations to go, James always seeing Marian safe home on these occasions.

" There, my dears, you mustn't go without taking a little something warm. Port wine negus—I know that's what will do you good. Don't shake your heads; you remember I'm a regular medical myself, and never prescribe wrong. And you going out into the night air, which if it isn't cold is sure to be damp, and if it is not damp is sure to be cold, and may take upon your chest, and lay you both up!—and then how about Hampton ? "

Having been almost compelled—at any rate prevailed upon to stop, and pay this purple libation to the Lares and Penates of Mrs. Bartlett's hospitable mansion, the lovers at last take their departure.

" Good night, my dear," says Mrs. Bart-

lett to Marian, as she gives her a good hug
and kiss at the door, " Good night, my dear,
and God bless you "—more kisses—" and
as for you "—addressing James—" I could
almost kiss you, too, if I could reach so
high, for you're a downright dear, that you
are; and why shouldn't I, for you're just
such another as my boy might have been,
if it had pleased God spare him."

James stooped down and kissed the good
woman's hand reverently. It was a hard
and not very small hand, but it was one
that had done many and many a good
action, and never grasped money too tightly
to let the poor have an alms out of its
earnings.

Then James and Marian turned their faces
northward, and set out arm-in-arm in the
direction of the latter's lodgings. When
they came to Regent Circus, there was a
temporary block, and they could not cross
the road for a minute or so. Cabs, omni-
buses, carriages, and carts were at a dead-
lock, owing to a slight complication—not
to say altercation—between the driver of a
Waterloo 'bus and the man belonging to a
van loading at the Bull and Mouth railway
office.

James and Marian waited at the corner of the pavement opposite Swan and Edgar's. A cab, with a large box on the roof, was brought to a standstill just in front of them. They were, however, too busily engaged in that absorbing conversation for which lovers are never at a loss to take any notice of the vehicle or its occupants, until a red-faced gentleman, with a grayish moustache, put his head out of the window and began to abuse the cabman.

"Curse you, why don't you drive on ? You'll miss the train, you sleepy-headed idiot, and lose the money I promised you. Curse it, go on !"

Marian looked up, glanced at the other occupant of the cab, and gave a start.

"What is it, dearest?" asked James, who felt her hand tighten its hold on his arm.

"That lady, in that fly ! It's Miss Orr, my late employer's daughter—Mrs. Henry Vorian !"

"And is that Henry Vorian !" asked James in a whisper.

"No; I don't know who it is."

"And they are going by rail ! Well, it's very odd," says James but just at this minute that *Deus ex machinâ,* a policeman, having accidentally appeared on the scene, the difficulty between omnibus and van is promptly solved, and the circulation of the traffic is resumed. The cab bearing Mrs. Vorian and the Major drives on, and is forgotten by both James and Marian in their happy talk of the future.

The next day, James is up betimes, and after breakfast hastens to the place appointed for their meeting by Charles Crawhall. It is a little sporting public-house near Drury Lane, and in front of it stands a very knowing-looking gray mare, in a high dog-cart. Charlie Crawhall is standing on the pavement, flicking off imaginary flies on the door panels.

The two Latrowes, attired in the height of slangy sporting fashion, are smoking cigars and putting on dog-skin gloves of great brilliancy.

" What's the meaning of this, Charlie ? " asks James, shaking him warmly by the hand, and nodding rather distantly to the Latrowes.

" Meaning ? why it's Hampton Races, Jim, and I'm going to do a sketch of it for Latrowe's new paper, *The Sporting Mercury and Theatrical Advertiser;* and they are going too. So jump up—you needn't go to the races, if you don't like—we can put you down at the house, and you can join us when you choose."

James was not very well pleased at the idea, nor was he quite satisfied with Charlie's share in the business. It was evident Crawhall had concealed the real object of his trip, and the fact that the Latrowes were going, for fear James should decline his offer.

"There, don't look glum, Jim," said the other, hustling him out of hearing of the others; "we shall have a nice drive and a good luncheon at their expense; and you and I'll sit in front, and make the two cads jump up behind!"

"But you know what scamps they are. I wonder you undertake to do anything for them; they won't pay you."

"Oh, won't they, though? You see, I've made a special study of them, and I find the poor rogues have no originality—they always cheat on the same plan. They pay —and handsomely—for the first job you do, and then try and get credited for the next and all subsequent ones. They throw a good-sized sprat this time ; but I'm blessed if their salmon is such a fool as he looks. Don't they wish they may catch him ? "

With these words, Charlie mounts the box, and makes James take the seat by his side. The two Latrowes scramble up behind, and try to sit as if they were very comfortable, and greatly in the habit of riding through life in dog-carts. They wear light coats, white hats, fancy waist-coats, white neckcloths, with horse-shoe pins, tight cord trousers, and highly-polished boots. They carry canes, and suck at very large and rather rank cigars, and swear profusely, which they consider is gen-tlemanly, and calculated to impress the world at large with their importance.

The dog-cart sets off, amid a small cheer volunteered by two crossing-sweepers, a newspaper boy, and a shoeblack — the latter probably joining-in out of purely professional admiration of the polish on the boots occupying the back seat.

There is no need to describe the road to Hampton, or to tell you how delightful a drive it is to that pleasant little village on the banks of the Thames. On this occasion, James Trefusis was not particularly struck

with it, for the road was crowded with
vehicles of all sorts, sizes, shapes, and de-
scriptions, their occupants being very noisy,
obstreporous, and much addicted to per-
sonality and practical jokes of a rough
character. All the lowest and worst features
of the Epsom road on Derby Day were here
vulgarly caricatured and exaggerated.

Gaudily dressed women lolled impudently
in carriages driven by flagrant gents. Cos-
termongers, prize-fighters, and the most
degraded specimens of the degraded race of
betting sharpers were thick as thieves—and
there was plenty of *them!*

It was a dull day, with a promise of the
recurrence of the heavy showers which had
fallen in the night. But the pinchbeck
swells who adorned the festivity clung to
their blue and green veils, and wore dust-
coats to keep the mud off. The whole affair
was to the Derby what Seven Dials is to
Piccadilly.

James was not at all sorry when Charlie
pulled up and directed him to the house he
was in search of, situated a short distance
down a lane turning out of the main road.

"You'll find us easy enough when you
want. We won't lunch till you come; but

don't stop too long, or I won't be sure that the hot weather won't open some of the champagne," shouted Charlie.

James was some little time before he could obtain admission to the house when he found it, for the man who had the care of it had started off to see the races, but was luckily overtaken, and brought back by a boy from a neighbouring cottage, whom James sent to find him.

The house was a pleasant place enough, with a view along the river, and a nice large garden. The rent was not exorbitant, and the whole was in capital repair.

James was so satisfied with it that he was prepared to close the bargain at once; but the man told him that he could not make any arrangement. Persons desirous of taking the house must communicate with Messrs. Pugh and Praysham, auctioneers, agents, and appraisers, of Hugh Street, Knightsbridge.

It had been James's intention to spend as much of his time as possible in inspecting the premises, for he did not care to be present at the orgies which are the chief feature of the Hampton Races. But his cicerone was so evidently on thorns to get

away, and had so plainly set his heart upon
seeing the fun of the course, that James
could not, as a question of humanity towards a suffering fellow-creature, detain
him longer than he could help.

So, when the released servitor had departed like a shot from a gun, James found
that there was nothing left but to follow
him at leisure.

He had reached the course, and had
already sighted Charlie Crawhall's dog-cart,
when an incident occurred which drove him
away from the scene in horror.

I have already said that these races are
a disgraceful and disreputable saturnalia,
indulged in by the lowest only, and shunned
by respectable people. The greatest license
reigns, and the fun is of the sort which is
thought very fine at an inferior country
fair.

As James was walking along, some one,
coming quietly behind him, drew across his
shoulder one of those common toys that
make a noise like the tearing of a coat. He
turned round with a start; the joke was
successful, and considered so exquisitely
humorous by those who saw it, that loud
and prolonged laughter followed it. The

performer of the trick was a flashily-dressed young man, who had a young girl upon his arm. James was about to speak angrily to the man, when his eye caught the face of the girl, who at the same moment recognised him.

"Good God! what are you doing here? What is the meaning of this?" James asked hoarsely, stretching forward and catching the girl by the arm.

It was Alice!

There—in such company—in that tawdry finery, with that blurred and blotted beauty, a face where the grace of innocence was wanting, and eyes that had no shame in them —it was impossible for her to seem anything else to James than what she really was. She cowered in terror, clinging to the arm of her companion, who stood a little bewildered before James's evident distress and horror.

"Oh, take me away—let me go!" she cried out. But James held her by the wrist.

"Tell me I am mistaken—tell me I am mad!" he hissed out. "But no! It is only too true—wretched, miserable girl— unhappy creature—poor, unhappy, wronged Alice."

"Let me go—take me away!" was all she could moan.

"No, come with me!" said James, trying to lead her away; "come to your sister—to Marian, who is so longing to see you!"

At the mention of Marian's name Alice shuddered, and with a sudden effort escaped from his grasp. Slipping behind her companion, she cried, "Keep him off! Don't let him take me!"

"Come, leave the girl alone!" said the man.

"Aye, leave the girl alone! What are you after? Go along!" came menacingly from the crowd which had gathered round.

"Stand back," said James sternly, "out of the way, fool! I will take her away from this cursed place."

"Go it, Jack, we'll stand by you!" said the friends of the little gent, pushing up to him, and placing themselves between James and Alice.

"Will you stand aside? Now or never! For by Heaven I'll knock you down," said James savagely.

The little gent, backed up by his friends, refused to move. Alice shrieked, imploring them not to touch James. But the crowd was a ruffianly crowd, and wanted to see a row.

And they did see it. For James Trefusis's left darted out, and down went the little gent. The next minute half a dozen had sprung at once on the young Cornishman. He had the knack of wrestling as well as fighting though, and several of them promptly measured their length on the sward. But numbers will overpower a giant, and it was lucky for James, who stood like a lion at bay, with half a dozen curs clinging to him, that the police came up and put a stop to the fray.

He explained to the sergeant the cause of the fight, and begged his assistance in rescuing Alice. But she had disappeared; and though James searched everywhere on the course, he failed to find any trace of her.

He returned to town sad and dispirited— almost heart-broken to think that it was his fate to tell the woman he loved what shame had come to her sister.

CHAPTER VI.

THE CAPTURE OF CRŒSUS.

MR. CHARLES FINK is one of the industrious classes. He is active and intelligent, and not altogether unpossessed of the advantages and experiences which can only be procured by foreign travel. He has seen the kangaroo bounding over his native plains, and has had opportunities of studying the floral beauties of a land so luxuriant in respect of them that the particular inlet where he sojourned had been actually called Botany Bay.

I regret to say that Mr. Charles Fink was not a wealthy man. His travelling expenses had been subscribed by the tax-paying community, on that splendid principle of legislation which enacts that if A robs B of a pocket handkerchief or purse, B, together with C, D, and other unoffending persons, shall club together to keep A in every luxury for a certain period, which shall be longer or shorter in proportion as the sum which B originally lost shall have been larger or smaller.

So, despite his having made the grand tour, and notwithstanding his having been educated and brought up at public expense, Mr. Charles Fink, *alias* Charley Fink, *alias* Flash Charles, *alias* the Cly-faker, *alias* the Yokel—all distinguished people are known to an admiring public by a *sobriquet* or antiphrasis of endearment—was by no means a prosperous individual.

To speak the plain truth, he was as miserable a vagabond as ever skulked on this earth, and lived just such a hand-to-mouth wretched life as the veriest cur that lurks about a butcher's market on the chance of offal. He was, to say it out at once, a thief.

Now a thief, in spite of that romantic life of "Jack Sheppard," and the shoal of cheap (and nasty—and what is more, inferior) imitations of it now published in weekly numbers for the edification of the youthful mind, is anything but a hero and a jolly dog. He works hard—very hard in a feverish, unwholesome way—at his

precarious avocation, and no man earns,—
as a mere abstract equivalent of money for
labour, apart from considerations of *meum*
and *tuum*,—so little by his labour. He is
known and noted by the police—a body
possessed of just sufficient intelligence to
enable them to keep their eye on a man
when he is down. And I know nothing
that more clearly points out the abject state
of the thief than the dull, unresisting way
in which he submits to capture, which a
little cunning, a little spirit, or even a little
capital, might enable him to avoid. He
skulks about by dusk and daylight, lives in
dens where only the poorest of the poor live,
and is pursued by constant terror, which
prevents him from enjoying his pitiful
plunder whenever he is fortunate enough to
get a haul. I speak of the thief, it must
be remembered. The skilled burglar is just
a step above him; but even his life is far
from being enviable.

But it is time I should close this little
essay upon " Rascality considered as a Profession," and resume my story.

Mr. Charles Fink having become dimly
conscious by a sort of brute instinct—for he
has never had the luck to be called on to

pay his rent quarterly—that this is the morning of Lady Day, has betaken himself in the direction of Lombard Street, where he intends to exercise his calling as opportunity may offer. He has been called "The Yokel," not because he can assume the appearance of a countryman, but because he happens to look like one—and I think this very unflattering reason will be found to hold good for all thieves' nicknames. So on this morning he loiters in Lombard Street as if he were a country cousin come to cash a cheque.

But he has not so lounged for a quarter of an hour, during which period nothing more lucrative than a bandanna falls in his way, when he happens to cast his eye up Babel Court, and espy a short man and a tall man who are taking the air in that cheerful *cul de sac*.

Mr. Fink's air changes in a minute. His apathy gives place to activity, and he hurries away from the neighbourhood as if he had suddenly recollected an appointment, and was ten minutes late already.

He only pauses once near a bank which is doing a brisk stroke of business, and he pauses there, not to exercise his calling, but

III.   G

to whisper to a widow lady, who is apparently in this quarter on business connected with the dividends.

" Bet, there's Bunce and Dodgett on the walk. Hook it ! " says Mr. Charles Fink; and the respectable widow immediately hails a passing omnibus, and insists on being taken to Camden Town. I regret to believe that two ladies in that omnibus found subsequently that their pockets had been picked,—and the respectable widow lady was not one of them.

Bunce and Dodgett are members of the Detective Police Force, and they were by no means concerning themselves about the doings of Flash Charles and Bet, the Brummagem Widow. Those worthies might have robbed a Director of the Bank of England under their very noses and escaped; for you could hardly expect the police-mind to be capable of thinking of two things at once; and they had one very serious and important matter already in hand.

But Charles Fink and Elizabeth the Relict having even a lower order of intelligence than Bunce and Dodgett, were kept in awe by those officers. You need not set a thief to catch a thief in these matters.

You only want one fool to look after a bigger fool.

Charles and Elizabeth then depart on their way, and Bunce and Dodgett still maintain their outward air of mystery, and perambulate Babel Court. The two former only appear for so brief a space on the stage that I may be pardoned for saying that I am sorry they were not aware of the preoccupation of the two latter, for then they might have found some work to do, poor creatures, and I might have found a further contribution to my essay "On Rascality considered as a Profession."

Whether any casual passenger up Ludgate Hill at about midday on the Lady Day I speak of observed the Cathedral of St. Paul's oscillate, or whether any traveller bound to London Bridge saw the Monument on Fish Street Hill tremble to its base, I cannot confidently assert; but there was an earthquake in the City on that day.

Pale men 'upon 'Change' whispered to others, "Have you heard?" "No; what?" "About old Orr?" "No. Nothing bad, eh?" "Rather!" "What, gone?" "I believe you!" "How much?" "Not known." "You don't say so?" "A fact,

sir. Had it from Smith, who was there
when they suspended." "By Jove!"

So the news spreads in a whisper. The
weather is a topic for once entirely neglected.
Mr. Orr's name is in everybody's mouth.

Yes! The clay feet of the golden idol
have crumbled to their native dust, and the
huge image lies prone. And at such a fall
well might St. Paul's Cathedral have shaken
and the Monument trembled.

Just as you have seen the fall of a high
wall, or a bridge or any other such huge
structure of masonry, so was the fall of
Mr. Orr. First comes the great crash; and
then, before the dust has cleared off, smaller
portions give way and drop into the general
ruin. Within two or three hours of Mr. Orr's
suspension, other houses had closed their
doors, and the panic was spreading. The
City, looked at from a certain point of view,
is only a row of card houses. Touch one,
and the chances are that half of the rest will
tumble down with it. It is a very humili-
ating picture of that great centre of wealth
and commerce, but it is a terribly true one.
I think City men must walk about holding
their breath for fear of bringing the frail
structure about their ears.

By about two or three o'clock, the whisper that runs through 'Change assumes a more awkward form. "I say, have you heard the last?" "What, about Orr's failure?" "More than that." "Nonsense! I haven't heard it then." "He's been arrested for forgery!"

Whereupon the informed gave such a whistle as some of my readers, I fancy, are indulging-in mentally.

Men shook their heads and looked grave at this; and some, I do not doubt, felt exceedingly unwell, for they possibly had skeletons in their strong boxes, and shook to think how slight a touch might reveal the secret, and place them in the same position as Mr. Orr. At which thought I dare say they got so angry with the man whose detection had suggested it, that they went away and told their friends what a pity it was that they did not hang for forgery now!

Mr. Orr's suspension was a work of small time. The order to stop payment was issued. The porter closed the door, the clerks put on their hats and departed; and Mr. Orr and his cashier, with one or two old and trusted servants who stood by him instinc-

tively rather than from any sense of personal
loyalty, were left to stare one another in the
face rather blankly in his dim inner sanctum,
where, it being a darkish day, the gas was
burning with a sickly look, as if it were
rather afraid the company would only get
twopence in the pound—which, by the way,
was a good deal more than they deserved
for the article they supplied.

At various periods of this day—and for
many days previous—Mr. Orr had peered
nervously over his wire blind into the narrow alley, wherein a tall man and a short
man had of late taken to disporting themselves. He has on one occasion had the
policeman on that beat called into his sanctum, and has ordered him to keep his eye
on these two men as suspicious characters,
who have been lurking about for some days,
evidently for no good purpose. The constable, with a stupid grin, agrees as to their
object, and promises to have them under
surveillance. But Mr. Orr, peeping furtively
through the blind after his departure, sees
him speaking on the most friendly terms to
the ill-assorted pair of watchers. They
thrust their tongues into their cheeks, and
shake with inward mirth.

On this particular afternoon, soon after
the suspension of payment is announced,
a military-looking man, in a tight blue frock
—an inspector of police, in short—appears
at the entrance of Babel Court, in company
with a thin, dry, parchmenty-looking gentleman, who gives you the impression that he
is a Darwin development of a weasel or a
ferret, and who carries a blue bag, bulgy
with papers. The inspector, having attracted
the attention of Bunce and Dodgett, goes
through the pantomime of taking the developed weasel into custody (much to that
acute individual's delight), and then indi-
cates Mr. Orr's premises with a jerk of his
thumb. Bunce and Dodgett nod and grin
likewise. It seems to be an excruciatingly
good joke.

When Mr. Orr has examined the books,
and had a talk with the cashier, and written
a few letters, he reaches down his hat from
its peg, takes a furtive glance over the blind,
and makes for the door. He opens it hur-
riedly, and goes out as if he meant to run
out of Babel Court. But he sees Bunce and
Dodgett standing in the entry, and pauses.
Then he walks deliberately towards them,
and they come forward to meet him.

The cashier, who had attended his employer to the door, sees this—sees the men accost Mr. Orr, and sees Mr. Orr stop. He thinks they are about to arrest the played-out capitalist for debt; he might be arrested now, for he has accepted the Chiltern Hundreds a week since. The cashier, worthy man, thinks it would be too painful for Mr. Orr to be arrested in this way; he himself has means, and will pay him out; so he hastens forward. He comes up to the group just in time to hear something about "forgery" spoken by the taller. Mr. Orr bows his head. There is something so shame-stricken and guilty in the action that the cashier turns back into the bank.

There is no yellow chariot waiting at the end of Babel Court to carry the great man back to Grosvenor Place. A common cab is hailed; they have not far to go, but it is an act of mercy to the prisoner. One policeman rides on the box; the other takes the front seat opposite Mr. Orr, and they drive off, the policeman on the beat grinning widely, and waving an adieu to Bunce and Dodgett. It is an act of taste and delicacy; but those are qualities for which the force is famed.

In a short time the ex-capitalist finds himself in no more cheering or comfortable a spot than a police-cell. He sinks down on his pallet, and begins to reflect for the first time calmly on what has happened, is happening, and will happen. In the last few days the fever has been too fierce, and he has not been able to think. Now that is all over, and he is collected.

He muses on the home once so grand and well-frequented, now tumbled in ruin around him.

But there are other homes which he has devastated. Not homes that were so seeming happy and prosperous as his, but which yet were far more contented and glad. At that moment, when he was sitting in his solitary cell, his name was on many lips—and it was uttered in bitterness, in anger—aye, with curses. And no wonder! How many had been misled by his sanctimonious hypocrisy into placing unbounded confidence in his integrity, and how many were now purchasing with the whole of their worldly riches the terrible experience that outward piety is a mere cloak for iniquity! They might have bought the knowledge cheaper, if I had only found time to print and

publish—and of course primarily to write—
that essay on " Rascality considered as a
Profession." For in that work, although
some considerable portion will be devoted
to the consideration of such poor scamps as
Charley Fink, I feel sure the greater number of chapters will have to be given up to
the big rogues—the Forger, who goes to
church regularly twice every Sunday—the
Robber of widows and orphans, whose name
appears in all the supscription lists of charities—the Dishonest Steward, who gives
(other people's) coals and blankets to the
poor at Christmas — with a host of such
other large varieties of the tribe *Raptores*.

Where is Mrs. Orr ?

She has been laid up ever since the day
when Captain Henry Vorian, bursting into
the room, suddenly announced the flight of
her daughter, his wife, and then launched
into a bitter diatribe against Mr. Orr and
his better half for selling their child to him
at the altar; with much more inconsequen-
tial raving, which might have been partially
true, but did not come with a good grace
from the other party in an infamous bargain.

Mr. Orr had borne the blow of Honoria's

flight far better than we might have expected until we learnt what has taken place now. A man who is about to submit to utter ruin and disgrace, who has the workhouse and a prison staring him in the face for his family and himself, can hardly be very sensitive about such minor details.

Mrs. Orr, I say, has not been well since she heard of her daughter's elopement. She was a mother in spite of all the hardening influences of money; and when she sat and sobbed over the girl's fate in her poor, common, vulgar way, she was a woman, instead of a doll stuffed with bank-notes, and stuck with diamonds.

But with Mr. Orr, when, as in duty bound, he confessed his embarrassments to her—and even revealed some portion of the forgery peccadillo—she was as hard and money-loving as it had been the labour of his life to make her.

"She would have nothing to do with him. She had money of her own settled on her, and she washed her hands of him. How dare he disgrace her in this way? What did he mean by dragging her down like this?"

You would have supposed, to hear her,

that she had brought him a large fortune and a distinguished name.

So Mr. Orr is deserted and solitary. The only friend he has is a lawyer, who comes to undertake the management of his defence. Lawyers are a much-abused body, and no one ever says a good word for them; and yet no man falls so low but that a lawyer will come to him and try and console him. When all the rest of the world had abandoned Mr. Orr, lo! here comes a lawyer to befriend him. In the debtor's room, in the murderer's cell, in the forger's cage, we find the lawyer always present. Why should we speak ill of a class so kindly, so beneficent, so unflinching? Why should we aim all our petty shafts of satire, all our small sneers and unchristian jokes, at a body of men who will not scruple to visit the most criminal among us in the most miserable dungeon, and who will strain every nerve, and employ every artifice, to clear the guilty wretch or mitigate his punishment—for a consideration?

CHAPTER VII.

MARIAN TAKES UP HER QUEST.

THERE comes a hum of busy voices from the open door of Marian's school. For the children are deeply engaged in their lessons, conning them off with all their hearts, because Teacher will shortly call them up to say what they speak of as their "jography."

It is a neat and clean little schoolroom this schoolroom of St. Pacifica's, and is pleasantly situated. It has a good-sized gravel yard behind, surrounded by back gardens belonging to the class of people who combine utility with elegance, and grow scarlet-runners and wallflowers. They also wash at home; and the display of linen, if clean, is coarse, and occasionally dilapidated. The gentlemen connected with the gardens frequently sit in them in their shirt sleeves of an afternoon, and smoke long clay

pipes with a fixed idleness—gazing hard at
some particular brick, or stump, or plant, and
thinking of nothing at all. The ladies clink
about on pattens, festoon their dab-washes,
and stimulate the infants who are not at
school into long howls, produced by the
smart application of a soap-suddy palm to
the cheek in the region of the eye, which
generally comes in for a touch of the sapo-
naceous that makes it tingle and weep. Cats
are prevalent on the garden walls, and these
form the sole distraction which can lure the
male inhabitants from the fixed idleness
I have mentioned. For those gentlemen
generally possess a dog, more or less
mongrel in breed, which they set at the
cat; and its disappointed yelpings, as pussy
glides off far above its reach, wake all the
neighbouring curs to clamour.

The *locale* is, in short, a struggling, respectable, hard-working suburb. There is
something very like real fresh air blowing
in at the windows from over the garden
space, and it brings the odour of wallflowers
and the smell of beans in bloom very often.
There is beside the gravel yard a field hard
by, where building operations have been begun and suspended. Here the children play;

and here, in the pools of stagnant water, collected where foundations have been dug, they catch sticklebacks with a worm and a bit of cotton; and sometimes, I regret to say, bring them into school in furtive pickle-bottles.

The neighbourhood is so quiet and out-of-the-way, in fact, that the appearance of a hansom there brings out half the inhabitants to their doors. The gentlemen lay down their pipes, take a last look at the object of their fixed contemplation, as if with a view to its identification on their return, and then come out to the doorway and stare. The small children, too small to go to school, scramble out into the road, at the imminent risk of being killed—either as if they did not know the nature of hansom cabs, and thought they could not run over people, or else in order to achieve fame by offering themselves as sacrifices to the first cab that had ever penetrated to that region. The ladies, who come clattering forth to inspect the phenomenon, are so absorbed in contemplation of it that they do not notice the peril of their offspring.

It is a yellow hansom, with a gray horse. Now a yellow hansom is a conspicuous and

beautiful object at any time or in any place
—I must confess that until quite recently,
when age had matured judgment, I never
could see a yellow hansom without feeling
a devouring passion to ride in it—so that,
apart from its novelty, there was some
ground for the sensation which the cab was
creating. The sensations of the passenger
in that vehicle, however, I should presume
were anything but pleasant. The road was
in a fearful state. Large horses, dragging
heavy loads of bricks, had poached it into
deep ruts and holes, and the mud had dried
into a sort of rugged rock now, so that the
gray horse stumbled and plunged fearfully,
and the yellow hansom rocked and oscil-
lated to the verge of an overturn. First
one wheel went into the rut, then the
other; then they both went with a jerk
and a bound over the barrier of an inter-
secting rut. And a hansom is just the
last sort of vehicle one would select for a
rough journey, on account of its lowness.
Bump, bang, roll, shudder, thump, bang!
No wonder the gray horse shook his head,
as much as to say, "Poor fellow, I know
he must be mad, or he would never come
along here!"

Meanwhile cabby, so far from being crazy, was quite sane enough to feel he had better abandon the affectation of a universal knowledge of locality, of which, as a rule, a London hansom cabby would sooner die than confess an ignorance. He was completely strange to these parts, and did not hesitate to admit it. So he kept asking the people he passed to direct him to some place which sounded very like "Sam Spiffiker's."

The natives wondered, but could not help him. They did not know any one of the name of Samuel Spiffiker anywhere thereabouts. At last the occupant of the hansom enlarges the inquiry by asking about "schools." They know the schools, but there's no one of the name of Spiffiker there. "Teacher's name's Carlyle," says one small urchin, who has had a week's schooling once.

James Trefusis—for it is he who is driving down into this strange region—immediately offers to give the youngster sixpence and a ride in the hansom, if he will act as guide to the schools.

James has frequently convoyed Marian to her lodgings, which are some little way

III.   H

from the school, so that his ignorance is
excusable. He had never been there, and
until now never had any reason to go.
What is the reason now ?

The reason is that all night long he has
been haunted by Alice's face. He has
heard the clocks chime round from midnight
till early dawn—and then has fallen into a
feverish sleep, troubled with dreams in
which Alice's face has appeared and re-
appeared, like the face of a corpse carried
down some rapid and turbulent stream.
He made up his mind at last to go straight
to Marian, and tell her what he saw at
Hampton—and he meant to go early, and
catch her at her lodgings ere she had left
for school. But towards morning he falls
into something like sound and refreshing
slumber, and when he wakes it is too late to
find her at home. So he determines to drive
to St. Pacifica's Schools, because having
once made up his mind that she is to be
told, he feels he shall never rest until she
knows all.

So, after much circuitous driving and a
great deal of direful jolting, thanks to the
urchin who gives his instructions to James,
who, in turn, conveys them to the driver

through the trap in the roof, the cab is at last safely piloted to the school-house.

" Run in doors, and tell teacher a gentleman wants to see her particularly."

The boy does as he is told, receives his sixpence, and goes away smiling and much envied—not only as the possessor of a silver coin of the realm, but also on account of his having ridden in a hansom.

Marian guesses who her visitor is, and sends word that he can walk up. She herself stands smiling at the head of the stairs; for she supposes that James has come to tell her that he has secured the house at Hampton, or some such pleasant news. But she sees the cloud on his face, and hers darkens immediately.

" What is it, James ? Ill news ?"

" Sore news, my darling. Make your heart strong to bear it, for it has nearly broken mine to learn it."

" What is it about, James ? About you ?"

" No, my child. But about some one very dear to us both."

" Alice ! " gasps Marian, and sinks down into her seat. ·They have walked up the schoolroom to her post. James leans over the desk before her.

"Tell me what you know, James!" she says, imploringly, as soon as the first stupor of dread passes off.

And then James Trefusis told her all that had happened at the races at Hampton the day before. But before he does so Marian dismisses the children, who get an hour's holiday, and are quite delighted at it, little knowing how sad the reason of their release is.

When she has heard the story with breathless impatience, she sinks her head upon her hands, and continues for a time weeping and praying silently. She remains awhile lost in thought. Then she gets up and comes round the desk to take James by both hands. She looks him long and mournfully in the face.

"Oh, James, it will break my heart! it will break my heart!"

Then she falls on his bosom, and weeps wildly and bitterly for a time, and he does not know how to comfort her. She can only repeat, "It will break my heart! it will break my heart!"

By-and-by this paroxysm of grief passes, and she grows calmer.

"Let me sit down and think, James.

Ah, my poor, poor child, my bright darling! What shall I do?" And once more her fortitude gives way, and she wrings her hands, and moans and weeps.

Then she springs up—"I must go and find her. I must go at once."

"Wait awhile, darling, be quiet awhile, and you shall go," says James, gently detaining her.

She sits down again. She is very docile —the truth being that for about half an hour the shock is too powerful for her brain, and she does not quite know what she is saying or doing.

At last, however, she recovers herself. She has wept all she may now, for it is time to decide what she shall do. She is again lost in thought. James has walked away, not to distress her by watching her sorrow. He is pretending to look out of the window.

"James," she says softly, coming up to him after a time, and laying her hand on his arm.

"My own one," he says, turning to her, and offering to clasp her to his heart—but she will not let him.

"You believe I love you?" she asks.

"I know it!"

"Yet we must part, James."

"Good heavens, what is the meaning of this? Has not our one parting been sufficiently bitter!"

"It must be, James. I cannot and will not let you suffer. With this shame come on me, I can be no man's wife."

"Shame on *you*, darling? What has this to do with you? We both mourn for a sister who is dead. But it is no shame to us."

"You may not think so, but others will. No! My purpose is fixed. I cannot be your wife now."

"Do you wish to drive me mad?"

"Oh, darling, darling, only love! Cannot you see it breaks my heart to say this? Cannot you love still as you would if I were dead? For I must be dead to you and to myself, to everything save the trust my dead father left me."

"Oh, Marian, I have toiled and waited so long. I have lost you and found you again. I have suffered sorely. Can you leave me thus?"

"Darling, James, it is my love for you that makes me see how impossible it is that your wife should bring a disgrace like this as a wedding dower."

"Oh, Marian, Marian, will you not learn that I care for nothing in the world but you—that without you the world is hateful to me? Be my wife!"

"I dare not, James. I must go and find my poor lamb. I will live on bread and water, and go clad in rags, but I will find her. I must find her—I shall find her at last, for I'll never cease searching this great city night and day."

"Be my wife, and we will search together."

"No, James! I must go on my mission —I must do my duty—alone. I will find her, or just lie down and die, when I've searched all I can, and yet seen no trace of her."

"But when you find her, Marian—will you come back to me, and be my wife then?"

"Will you let me, after all I shall have had to pass through? Will you let me, with her with me? No, you *must* not. I know you, James, and I feel sure you would, but it must not be."

"But I may see you?"

"Oh, James, it would unnerve me for the work. But I'll write to you."

"And this is your firm and unalterable resolve?"

"Yes, James, my own love. Don't break my heart with struggling against it. Suffer it for my sake—for your sake—for hers!"

"God help me—and bless you!"

"Good-bye, my own, own love!" She sprang to his arms, clung round his neck, and kissed him.

"Good-bye, darling of my heart!"

And so, striving to find in poor words an expression of what they felt, they took leave of each other.

CHAPTER VIII.

HOW THE LACQUOIGNES BEAR IT.

I DO not envy the Honourable Henry Vorian his house in Kensington after the departure of his wife. They had quarrelled, it is true, and avoided one another, while she was with him. But now the utter silence of the house—for the servants crept about it silently like scared ghosts, or wild creatures before a storm — the unbroken and awful stillness seemed as though Death had set up his habitation there.

But the silence was more terrible than that which death brings to a household. It was the silence of dishonour.

Even the nursery was deserted. For as soon as the flight of Honoria was reported at the house in Grosvenor Place, Mrs. Orr ordered out the yellow chariot, drove to Kensington, and carried off both child and nurse. I do not know by what right she did this, but she was accustomed to command, and happening to arrive during Henry's absence, she gave her orders with such calm consciousness of strength that no one ventured to oppose them—not even Charles, though his eye was still adorned with an Iris that should have held out to him an ominous promise of what was likely to happen if he were an unresisting spectator of more elopements from his master's house.

But Henry was not at all disposed to quarrel with Mrs. Orr for carrying off the child, or with Charles for permitting her to do so. He was only too glad to be relieved of the encumbrance. Besides, the child was too like his mother to be pleasant company. Nevertheless, the absence even of his fretful wails made the silence of the house more deep.

Nobody came near Henry. People did not quite know how far the story was true, or did not know what course to adopt if it were true—or didn't trouble their heads about it at all any further than to say that they had always thought that Vorian and his wife lived unhappily—that he was a

brute and she was a vixen, and both were
equally to blame.

As for my lord and my lady, they were so
utterly disgusted at the result of their son's
alliance with the daughter of a person of
obscure birth, that they retired forthwith to
Beaudechet.

It was quite curious to observe how
treacherous were their noble memories.
They were both under the impression that
they had " always been opposed to the
match—but poor Henry was so infatuated.
They had felt it was a *mésalliance*, and did
not like to see a member of their ancient
house marrying into the family of a mere
wealthy *parvenu*." I believe if it had been
possible for the aristocratic nose to turn up,
it would have curled with a double hitch, as
sailors say, at the mention of Mr. Orr's
name.   But unbending fate and an in-
flexible cartilage forbad such a protest.

Although the relations of Henry to his
noble parents had never been very warm
and cordial, he certainly missed them now.
He wandered about the echoing rooms of
his deserted home with a wild, restless
pacing like that of a caged wild beast.   He
had no one to consult or talk to; for he

was ashamed to tell his story to his legal adviser, except by letter.

There was nothing to be done. There were no active steps to be adopted, or he might have found relief in energy. But his wife had written a very cold, formal letter from the Continent, admitting her fault, and declaring her intention of never returning to England. So that Henry had not even the ghastly employment of accumulating proofs of his own dishonour.

At length it occurred to Henry to write to an old brother officer, and ask him to come and advise him. Accordingly, in the course of the next day or so, Colonel Armytage called upon him.

" My dear Vorian, I am most grieved for you. Distressed beyond measure, I assure you. Could hardly believe my ears when I heard of it. What can I do for you ? "

" What ought I to do, Armytage ? Curse the woman, I don't care about her. She may go to the deuce if she likes. He's heartily welcome to her, and a pretty life she'll lead him as a penalty. But you see, my honour, Jack—my honour ! What am I to do ? "

" Well, if you want my opinion, I think

you must shoot him. Do—upon my soul.
Can't see any other way out of it."

" There's nothing I should like better,
but in these days——"

" Why, you're not in the army now.
They can't come down upon you for duel-
ling against the regulations."

" But the general opinion is so strong
against it, Jack. I'm not afraid, you know
—for I'm a good shot, and should dearly
like to shoot the dog. But then, now-a-
days, one's tried for murder for these
things, and I'll be hanged if I should like
to be hanged for such a woman."

" Where are they ? Not in England, I
suppose ? "

" No, on the Continent."

" The very thing—follow them there, and
call him out. Nobody takes any notice of
duels abroad."

" By Jove, the very thing. Egad, I'll
start to-morrow."

" By the way, old fellow—you'll pardon
me—but who is the man ? There are so
many rumours."

" That blackguard Cantlow."

" What ! Major Cantlow ? "

" That's the man ! "

"Then, my dear fellow, you may save yourself the trouble and expense of a trip to the Continent."

" Why ?   What do you mean ? "

" Mean !   That he won't fight.   The fellow's a cur, and will not face you. You're not the first man who would like to get satisfaction out of Cantlow—but you will not be the last either, if that's any consolation."

" But he can't refuse ! "

" Won't he, though ?   You don't know Cantlow. But that is evident, or you would not have admitted him as a visitor. He's a regular black sheep,—and as cowardly ! How did you come to meet him ? "

" At the Orrs'."

" That comes of mixing in that sort of society.   I beg you pardon, though, old fellow, I forgot they are connections——"

" Not now, Jack ; so abuse them to your heart's content, and I'll be chorus."

" Can't see that it would do us any good. Wish you could get a chance of shooting him, though. But you won't. Know him too well to expect that !   Beggar was kicked out of the Rag ages ago for card-sharping."

" The deuce he was ! "

" Yes ! And what's more, some of the pigeons he had been plucking wanted him to go out, but he laughed at them."

"Then I suppose it is no use following him.   But, by George, if I ever meet him, I'll break every bone in his sneaking carcase."

" I'll tell you what I'd do, Vo., if I were you.   I'd shut up the house——"

" I mean to sell it."

" Very well, then sell it, or hand it over to your agents to sell for you, and go down into the country.   Your people are at Beaudechet, are they not ? "

" Yes, confound 'em ! "

" Well, go down there till this has a little blown over."

" By Jove, Jack Armytage, why didn't I think of that ?   It is just the thing, for if I stop here much longer all alone in the infernal echoing, empty house, I shall go crazy."

Accordingly, the next day found Henry Vorian and his luggage on the platform of the railway, waiting for the train to start. He had handed over possession of his house to Scrooby, and instructed him at the same time to take the necessary steps to procure a divorce.

It was evening, and the station was crowded with Government clerks and City men, all bound for their suburban and semi-rustic residences. There was a great scuttling to and fro of porters, ringing of bells, steam-whistling, and such cheerful sounds as seem to be inseparable from railway travelling—to wit, the loud successive banging of all the carriage-doors—the rattle and click of the axle-box lids, as the man with the box of pine-apple ice inspected them each in turn—the clang of the wheels as the unseen inspector, crawling beneath the carriages, sounded them all, one after the other, with a hammer.

Then there were the shrieks and complaints of elderly females, who were under the impression that this was or was not their train, and did not believe their luggage was right, and wanted to know how soon they would reach their destination, with a thousand other shrill queries or querelæ.

Henry Vorian did not, however, object to the noise and bustle; it diverted him.

"Paper!   *Ev'n Sta'd'd*, sec' deesh'n.
Star, or *Sta'd'd*, Paper!"

The boy came yelling past where Henry
was standing. He carried a bill of the
contents of one of the papers, and Henry,
almost without thinking, read it. It ran
thus :—

Evening Standard,

June 26th.

ALARMING CONFLAGRATION AT WAPPING.
LATEST INTELLIGENCE FROM PARIS.
ATTEMPTED MURDER AND SUICIDE AT GLASGOW.
SHOCKING MURDER AT RIPON.
ROBBERY AT LEEDS : CAPTURE OF THE BURGLARS.
FAILURE OF ORR'S BANK.
OUTBREAK IN THE SOUTH OF ITALY.

The Honourable Henry Vorian was
naturally not much interested in the fire
at Wapping. He did not know where that
place was, or anything about it; and he
certainly had no property there. The latest
intelligence from Paris, as it was not likely
to mention " the arrival of Major Cantlow
and the Honourable Mrs. Vorian at the
Hotel du Louvre," did not greatly interest
him. He thought little about the attempted murder and suicide at Glasgow—
unless, indeed, he made a passing conjec-

III.   I

ture that it might be a husband attempting to kill a faithless wife—nor was he deeply concerned about the murder at Ripon, or the robbery at Leeds.

But when he came to the "Failure of Orr's Bank," he was taken considerably aback. He could hardly believe his eyes.

"Here, stop! Give me an *Evening Standard*," he gasped.

"*Sta'd'd*, sir? Yes, sir," said the boy, giving him the paper, and pocketing the coin Henry gave him, with equal promptitude.

Henry at once took his place in the train, settled himself down in a corner, and proceeded to hunt for the paragraph about Orr's Bank.

With a trembling hand he cut the pages with his ticket, and at last discovered and read the brief announcement that "At an early hour this morning the doors of Mr. Orr's Bank in Babel Court, Lombard Street, were closed, and a notice posted up to the effect that it was compelled to suspend payment."

Henry Vorian put down his paper, and became lost in thought of anything but the most agreeable kind.

In the meantime three or four passengers entered the compartment where he was sitting and took their seats, and in a few minutes the train was in motion.

The new-comers were regular daily travellers by the line, living out of town, and coming to business by rail every morning and returning every evening. They were therefore acquainted with one another, and soon fell into a conversation, which presently turned upon a topic that made Henry Vorian prick up his ears.

"Deuce of a thing this smash of Orr's," said Mr. Badger, a spruce, dapper City man.

"Yes; very heavy, isn't it?" asked Mr. Moorsom, a Government clerk.

"Extent not known yet; but I'm afraid there'll be a whole lot of poor people ruined. He did a thundering big trade, you know. People had great confidence in him, he was so religious."

"Blessed old humbug! What's the cause of the smash—have you any idea?"

"None in the world. He had no business to break with such a large trade."

"Oh, you know," here broke in Mr. Lardie D'Ardour, who was a swell in the

Treasury; "Oh, you know, they say his son-in-law, Vorian, future Lord Lacquoigne, let him in heavily."

"Ah, that's the fellow whose wife ran away from him," said the City man.

"Yes; they say he treated her brutally," said D'Ardour. "She ran away with some officer in his old regiment."

"Ah, indeed!"

"Well, old Orr will survive the smash, I suppose," resumed Mr. Moorsom after a pause, during which the train had stopped at a station and taken in one or two additional passengers.

"You were speaking of Mr. Orr, of Orr's Bank, I presume?" said one of the new-comers.

"Yes," said Moorsom rather curtly, and with some hauteur, for he did not quite like being addressed by a perfect stranger—no Englishman ever does.

"Then I suppose you haven't heard the latest news?"

"Nothing later than the stoppage. Is there anything else than what's in the *Standard?*" broke in Mr. Badger.

"Oh, yes. In the latest edition I suppose it will be; but I heard it from a friend, who was transacting business with the lawyer for the prosecution "——

"Prosecution!" cried all.

"Yes, Orr's arrested on a charge of forgery."

The opening of the conversation I have chronicled was anything but pleasant to Henry Vorian, who was once or twice on the point of interfering to contradict some of the false rumours which the elegant but inaccurate Lardie D'Adour, was propagating. But when he heard of his father-in-law's being in custody for a crime, you may well suppose that he wished his journey at an end, or longed to be in a compartment by himself.

His musings, you may imagine, were anything but cheerful and satisfactory, and he was very glad indeed when a railway porter, shouting out something quite as difficult to spell as Houyhnhum is to pronounce, told him that he had arrived at the junction, whence another train would bear him to his destination.

The train sped onward with its human freight, the travellers in Henry's compartment little dreaming how closely their conversation had concerned him.

You cannot be too careful how you discuss general topics in a railway carriage. I remember a friend of mine once told me that he travelled from London to Edinburgh with a quiet, bald-headed, respectable old gentleman, and that they beguiled the greater part of the journey with a discussion about a case of embezzlement by a cashier, who had absconded with twenty thousand pounds after having already defrauded his employer to about the same amount. When they arrived at Auld Reekie, a man put his head into the carriage, and blandly informed the mild little gentleman that he was a detective, and that he must arrest him. And it turned out that my friend's new agreeable acquaintance was the absconding cashier himself, of whom, by the way, he had, my friend remembered, spoken throughout with severity tempered by charity and benevolence. I introduce this anecdote as a warning to travellers to be particular in their choice of topics for conversation.

Henry Vorian had startling intelligence for his noble parents when he reached home that evening. My lord turned blue at the news, and my lady scarlet.

" *This* comes," she said with some asperity, " of intermarrying with low people."

" Upon my soul, Henry," said his lordship, " I think I could almost congratulate you on your wife's flight, for it will enable you to sever all connection with the family."

" You would not congratulate me if you knew how busy scandal is with my name ; " and Henry repeated the remarks of Lardie D'Ardour ; whereat his lordship grew very wroth, and swore in his most forcible manner, to the great disgust of her ladyship.

But when the noble family of Lacquoigne began, on calm reflection, to survey the position in which they were left by the utter collapse of Mr. Orr, disgust began to give place to bewilderment.

What were they to do ? They had invested their son in the Marriage Mart, and the speculation had turned out a bad one, and unluckily he was not available for a second venture. And the House of Lacquoigne could not put up its shutters like the House of Orr, and issue a notice that it had suspended payment. It was so hard, too—just as good fortune seemed to be within their grasp, and for the first time in their lives these high-born beggars had known what it was to live comfortably and be free from the terror of debts and duns—that the whole fabric they had so industriously erected should crumble.

Well might the lofty trees in the Beaudechet avenue moan that night. They must be decimated to meet the emergency. How many of them, instead of flecking the greensward with dappled light and shade, must fall beneath the axe, and depart to assist in the manufacture of ships, coffins, furniture, firewood, and railway-sleepers! Well might the twinkling rabbits that flit and vanished in the dusky drives, tremble and cower in their hiding-places; for they were foredoomed to slaughter—a poor forlorn hope thrown forward to cut down the expenses. What cart-loads of them would be jolted to town to feed the vulgar million, instead of adorning the slopes and shades of Beaudechet.

Of course his lordship's creditors, on learning Mr. Orr's failure and arrest, do not forget to press their claims. They become painfully importunate. His lordship

begins to wish that there might be a rise in
the price of rabbits, or a large demand for
timber—or that it might become the fashion
to visit Beaudechet.   He is really almost
inclined to take a leaf from the book of the
enterprising proprietor of Cremorne, and
advertise, "This splendid baronial mansion
and its magnificent grounds open daily.
Great attractions!   New and varied entertainments!" He wants money so badly that
I verily believe, if he thought that it would
realise a profit, he would open his grounds
in this style, and even by way of supplying
amusement to the public, start exhibitions
of all sorts.   Imagine Lord Lacquoigne as
the Bounding Baron of the Bankruptcy
Court, making both ends meet; or her ladyship as the Phenomenon Peeress, balancing
her accounts on her aristocratic nose; or the
Honourable H. Vorian as the Champion
Swordsman, cutting down his expenses!

But we ought not to laugh at these poor
people's mishaps, even though they have
brought them upon themselves.

The privations of this noble family are
enough to touch the hardest heart. A peeress
dressed in a common print, in order to save
her silks; a baron shooting rabbits for a bare

subsistence; the heir of the house and title reduced to smoking a common clay pipe and coarse tobacco, because he cannot afford a havanna—these are spectacles which it is painful to contemplate.

But they are not so badly off as Mr. Orr, who finds, in spite of the numerous firm and unswerving friends who had so often publicly declared they would always be proud to stand by him, that he cannot get substantial bail, and is therefore still in custody.

CHAPTER IX.

COMMITTAL AND CONVICTION.

THERE is considerable excitement and a great deal of crowding at the Mansion House when Orr, the forger, is brought before the Lord Mayor.

James Trefusis manages to get a seat, and means to hear the case out. He is a little ashamed, I hope, inwardly, of the savage joy he feels at the disgrace that has befallen one who treated Marian so cruelly.

The Worshipful the Lord Mayor is anything but comfortable. He is not a powerful man mentally—I need hardly say that, after having admitted that he is a Lord Mayor—and he is a good-tempered, well-intentioned creature. He has certain social superstitions, one of the strongest of which is that one ought never to forsake a man beneath whose mahogany one's legs have reposed. This is one of the strongest of his superstitions, because it attacks him in one of his weakest points—his stomach. The man who has ever given him clear turtle has a lien on his—I was going to say " soul," but, on consideration, will substitute " gratitude." Now he had often sat at Mr. Orr's feasts, and was therefore horribly troubled internally—as if he had had a very bad dinner—at the thought of sitting in judgment on his Amphitryon.

When the prisoner is brought in, his Worship does not know whether he ought to bow to him or offer to shake hands with him ; so he pretends to have something to say of great importance to his clerk, and thus escapes the difficulty.

Mr. Orr is a terribly altered man. He appears to have grown thinner, and his usually rosy complexion is sallow. His dress looks neglected, and his hair unkempt. His old arrogance and magnificence of manner have disappeared. He crouches and stoops, and is already marked with the felon's brand. He looks no one in the face, but hangs his head down as if he were watching his nervous, fidgety fingers.

As he makes his appearance, there is a low, ominous murmur in Court. It is not a noise that the officers can suppress. It speaks very plainly that if the prisoner were in the hands of that crowd, he would get scant mercy. And small wonder! for that crowd is chiefly composed of the unfortunate people whom he has ruined, or well-nigh ruined—whom he has deceived by sham honesty, sham goodness, sham Christianity.

Mr. Louis, one of a well-known legal firm famous for their defences of desperate cases, is in attendance on behalf of the prisoner. The prosecution is conducted by a Q.C. His Worship is compelled to resign all hope of showing favour or mercy to his former host by the presence of the Q.C., which does great credit to his honesty and impartiality.

The evidence is simple enough. The forgeries are orders, cheques, and bills, purporting to be drawn by a mercantile firm in India. They represent a large amount, and extend over a brief and very recent period of time. After the Q.C. has shortly and succinctly opened the case, the chief witness is called, who is the head of the mercantile firm, and whose arrival in England was the signal for Mr. Orr's capture. This witness, on being shown the signatures, distinctly swears that they are not in his handwriting. Being pressed, he says that, to the best of his belief, they are in the handwriting of the prisoner, with whom he has corresponded on matters of business. They bear no resemblance to his (the witness's) handwriting.

Cross-examined : They do not appear to be imitations of his signature. He should say that no one who has been accustomed to see his signature would have been deceived by them.

Re-examined: He had always banked with the prisoner. His cheques and bills were generally sent to the prisoner, with whom he was in the habit of corresponding. Should think the prisoner might have been able to manage affairs so that his signature was never seen by any one but himself. (This question was objected to by Mr. Louis, but eventually allowed.) Believes that would be quite possible.

Mr. Louis put a question through the Court, to which the witness replied that he was not practically acquainted with banking business.

The second witness was Mr. Orr's cashier. He stated that he had been in the prisoner's employment fifteen years, and knew his handwriting well. The documents produced were signed by Mr. Tasker (the last witness), to the best of his belief. He had frequently noticed that the prisoner and Mr. Tasker wrote very similar hands. (Shown the signature of last witness.) Had never seen any writing of that sort before. If that was Mr. Tasker's handwriting, it was evident that the documents previously shown him could not have been signed by Mr. Tasker. Could not distinguish any difference between that handwriting and that of the prisoner. Would not swear it was the prisoner's. It was very much like it.

Mr. Louis cross-examined this witness with great severity, the drift of his questions evidently being to imply that the forgeries were committed by the witness. He elicited that witness had once been dismissed by Mr. Orr, but subsequently the dismissal was reversed.

Re-examined : The reason why Mr. Orr threatened to discharge him was because certain defalcations were detected, which Mr. Orr attributed to him. He was innocent, and the guilty person being subsequently discovered, tried, and transported, he of course retained his situation. He knew the prisoner's handwriting well, and had long been accustomed to examine handwriting with a view to guard against fraud. (The witness had been asked by Mr. Louis if he was a professed expert.)

The third witness was T. Bunce, a member of the detective police force, who deposed that, from information he had received, he took the prisoner into custody in Babel Court as he was leaving the bank. Prisoner asked him what the charge was; on which he informed him that it was for forging the signature of Mr. Tasker, of the firm of Clark, Tasker, and Phinn, of Calcutta. Prisoner said, "I thought so." Warned him that anything he said would be used against him on his trial, whereupon he said, "Thank you; I'll be on my guard." Searched the prisoner's room at the bank. Discovered a cheque-book (produced). The cheque marked A corresponded with one of the foils in that book. It was torn crookedly, and the edges corresponded. Found under the table a rubbish basket, in which were fragments of paper, torn up very small. Found, on fitting some of the pieces together, that the name of "George Tasker" had been written on a sheet of paper three or four times, as if for practice. The signature so written corresponded with the signature on the documents alleged to be forgeries. (The witness here handed up the joined fragments.) Also examined the blotting pad which was on prisoner's desk. Found a portion of a sheet of blotting-paper that had been torn away still adhering to the pad. On it was written " Geo. Tas "—the remainder of the signature was torn off. The writing resembled that on the forged documents. (The witness here handed up the blotting pad.)

Cross-examined: Had not been promised any reward. Thought it likely that he might get one. Did not know from whom. Other people might have used the rubbish basket. Other people might have used the blotting pad. (Mr. Louis placed in the witness's hand the joined fragments.) The signatures differed slightly. When he said they resembled those on the forged documents, he meant some of them did. The ink had run on the blotting-paper (handed to witness by Mr. Louis). It might be " Geo: Far." Was not aware that one of Mr. Orr's clerks was called George Farmer.

Re-examined: Should have done all he

did as a matter of duty, without any expec-
tation of reward. The rubbish basket was
in Mr. Orr's private room. So was the
blotting pad. The clerks in the outer office
had blotting pads and baskets for their own
use. Of the differing signatures on the
joined fragments, some appeared to him to
be in prisoner's ordinary handwriting;
others were in the same hand, a little dis-
guised. It was the latter that resembled
the signatures on the forged documents.
Whether the writing on the blotting-paper
was " Geo. Tas," or " Geo. Far," it was in
the same hand as that on the forged
cheques and on the joined fragments.

The last witness was an expert in handwriting, who, on being sworn, had all the
papers handed to him. He was of opinion
that the writing on the joined fragments
was the prisoner's. It appeared as if he had
been practising in order to disguise his
hand, and that when he had succeeded in
doing so to his satisfaction, he adopted the
signature for the forgeries. The writing at
the top of the joined fragments was exactly
like the prisoner's ordinary hand, as shown
in documents acknowledged to be his.
Those at the bottom were identical with the

signatures to the forged documents. The intermediate ones showed a slight resemblance to both. The writing on the blotting pad, when reversed in a mirror, was clearly " Geo. Tas." It was the same as that on the forgeries.

Mr. Louis cross-examined this witness closely as to his experience, and endeavoured to shake his testimony, but without avail.

The case for the prosecution having closed, Mr. Louis made a speech in defence. He alleged that there was no case at all, that there was nothing to connect the prisoner in any way with the forgeries, and that the only things approaching to anything that might implicate him in the most remote way were to be found in the evidence of a witness who admitted that he expected a reward for what he had done. The learned gentlemen then went into a detailed account of the prisoner's life and career, describing him as a man who had risen by his own exertions, honesty, and integrity to a distinguished position; who had been an ornament to Parliament; and as a private individual, had been distinguished for piety and benevolence. His

affairs, it is true, had become a little in-
volved of late, owing chiefly, he was instructed to state, to too generous a reliance
on the commercial integrity of others; but
this temporary embarrassment could not for
a moment be considered as likely to induce
a man of Mr. Orr's probity to forfeit the
advantage of a long life of honest industry
for the sake of a little money. Was it likely
that a man of his experience would have
had recourse to so clumsy a fraud—to put
it on the lowest ground? He (Mr. Louis)
had no wish to cast imputations upon any
one; but it was impossible to help asking
if there were not others connected with
the bank who had equal opportunities and
greater temptations? He was convinced
that his Worship would dismiss the case.

His Worship, after consulting with his
clerk for some time, said that he was deeply
pained and shocked to see a man in Mr.
Orr's position in life brought before him on
so grave a charge. It would have given him
sincere pleasure to dismiss the case, and
send Mr. Orr away without a stain upon
his character; but he felt he should not be
performing his duty as Chief Magistrate if
he did not do all in his power to have the

charge fully investigated. It was to Mr. Orr's interest, as well as the interests of justice, that a most searching inquiry should be made, and every tittle of the evidence carefully sifted. He could not help saying that there appeared to him to be quite sufficient evidence for the prosecution to warrant his sending it to a jury.

The prisoner was committed for trial accordingly, and being unable to procure bail, was removed in custody.

This is a brief summary of the newspaper report of the case. I need not go over the evidence again, as adduced at the trial. Suffice it that, in spite of an able defence by an able barrister, who has since been raised to the Bench, a jury of twelve of his countrymen were unanimously of opinion that Mr. Orr was guilty. He was sentenced to fourteen years' transportation.

Neglected by his former friends, deserted by his wife, forgotten by his children, the wretched man dragged out seven of the years of his cheerless captivity. At the end of that period his health appeared suddenly to give way. His constitution broke up rapidly, and though he was promptly removed to the hospital, he never recovered. His name has perished. His grave is unknown.

In this way one of those against whom James Trefusis registered a solemn vow of vengeance was removed beyond the reach of his wrath. When James Trefusis made that vow, it seemed an absurd one—so far beyond his power of injuring him did the great millionaire appear to stand. When that vow was cancelled, the poor, broken-down, faded, miserable convict was sunk too low for his revenge.

CHAPTER X.

WHEN James left her, Marian sat down in the schoolroom, which was very quiet now the children had dispersed, and, looking her trouble straight in the eyes, tried to read all it had to tell her. It was a painful task, but she felt she must do it. She was obliged to realise the whole truth of what James had told her. She had to face the awful knowledge that the sister over whose childhood she had watched like a mother—by whose innocent pillow she had knelt at the time of her bereavement to pray for strength to watch over her as a mother should—was another being now. It seemed to her as if Alice were older than she now.

Oh, the agony of surmising how the clear, pure light of those blue eyes had died out! It was almost impossible for Marian to realise the change that must have come over the girl she remembered in the happy days in the West. It is impossible for a good woman to conceive the full extent of such a change—how a once sweet nature so fallen revolts against everything that reminds it of the past, and plunges only the more deeply, the more hopelessly, into the dreadful present.

When Marian had forced herself to acknowledge what must have been the change in her sister, she began to plan out what her future course must be. She weighed everything carefully, for she knew it was no light task she was undertaking. At its very outset she would be beset by suspicion, misapprehension — insult possibly.

She could not conceal from herself how hopeless such a quest was. When she reached home that evening she looked out of the window of her room. Her lodgings were in one of the high-lying quarters of Islington, and she looked out over a black far-spread sea of roofs, stretching away on all sides under the lurid canopy that hung over it. In those endless miles of streets, whose glare flung that red light on the sky, how seemingly hopeless it was to think of finding her whom she was to seek.

There is something peculiarly depressing in the sight of London at night, viewed as Marian viewed it. The roar that comes up from it seems the realisation of "the howling of the wilderness" in Scripture. That hoarse sound is the combination of the noises—small and insignificant enough in themselves—of millions of lives, all going on their separate ways, utterly ignorant, entirely disregardful, of the unit that looks and listens, and despairs. Every word, every footstep, helps to form that tremendous aggregate; yet out of the myriads of voices, the myriads of feet, not one voice possibly speaks your name, not one foot seeks you.

It has always seemed to me that the sight of London by night from a little distance is enough to break any forlorn creature's heart with the inexorable knowledge of that worst isolation—isolation in the midst of an unending crowd of fellow-beings.

The sight was melancholy and dispiriting enough to Marian. She had often looked out upon it as one does upon the midnight

ocean when one is living by the seaside.   It
had filled her with awe and a sense of her
desolation and weakness.   But she had
looked upon it with curiosity rather than
active dread.

Now, however, the time was come when
she was to plunge into its cold, cruel
billows.   Her heart was strong to do it,
but it was hardly strange that she should
hesitate for one moment on the brink.

When the gallant fellows who man the
lifeboats along our coast hear the sullen
signal of distress booming over the breakers,
they are ready enough to launch the life-
boat and put out to save the shipwrecked.
But I dare say—I hope, indeed, for the
truest bravery is that which fully esti-
mates the peril it faces—I hope that as
those noble men leap into the brave boat,
they turn just one look to the cottage on
the cliff yonder, or the wife's pale face in
the crowd, or the bonny lass there, who is
down on her knees on the sand praying
for her lover.   I should think the better,
not the worse of them for that: it is a
part of the same tenderness of heart that
sends them out to face the storm for the
sake of the poor wretches out on the bar

yonder clinging to slippery spars and whistling cordage.

So when Marian, who is about to go out in this forlorn hope to save the shipwrecked sister, who is going down in this cruel sea, that spreads out inky black before her, we shall not doubt her because the tears are slowly flowing—because she turns a longing gaze to the figure of that big broken-down man, broken-down at the thought of losing her, but submitting to what she holds to be her duty. We shall not love her the less even because, having learnt to have a home in these humble lodgings—having spent her quiet, pleasantly melancholy and sorrowfully happy evenings here so long, she feels that she is taking a farewell of old friends. The two Chinese fans, the pair of China vases, the porcelain poodle, the little shepherd and shepherdess, the Art-Union engravings, the oil painting of her landlady's father even— all seem to be so many parts of home, all were her companions in the still evenings which are over now. She will never know again the calm and rest of the twilight hours, when duty was accomplished and the toil of the day was done.

This was the last evening she would spend at home. It was no idle sentiment that induced her to delay her task for the one night. She had to set herself right with one or two people before she took up her quest, and she felt she must do that first of all. That done, nothing could occur to hinder her or delay her search.

The first person she had to speak to was her landlady, Mrs. Warner.

Mrs. Warner was a tall, thin, elderly Scotchwoman, who had married the valet in the family where she had been "leddy's maid," as she called it. After their marriage, her master had procured her husband a messengership in one of the public offices, and she had set up a lodging-house. She was one of those hard, dry women who may be any age. Like parchment which is very new or very old, but between those two extremes may be of any age, these women are easily set down as gaunt girls or shrivelled old crones, but their years between those two ages cannot be in any way estimated.

Marian had always experienced the greatest kindness and consideration at Mrs. Warner's hands; but they were of that hard, angular sort, which prevents one from doing full justice to them. She had never been able to find out, in spite of her care and attention, whether Mrs. W. possessed a heart. Of course, she had the usual apparatus for the propulsion of the sanguineous molecules; but whether she had a metaphorical heart—the thing which is supposed to yearn to relatives, which is displayed with a skewer through it in valentines, and which is reported to suffer fracture at the hands of the faithless of the other sex—had been a mystery to Marian.

It was no easy task to tell her all that she must tell her, but Marian summoned up her fortitude and courage. She sent down word by the servant girl, who brought up the tray with her modest little bit of supper, that she should like to see Mrs. Warner presently if she were not engaged.

When Marian had finished her supper and rang to have it cleared away, Mrs. Warner herself answered the bell, and said she " understood Miss Carlyle wished to speak to her."

Marian asked her to take a chair, which she did when she had arranged the supper things ready for removal to her

satisfaction.   She took a chair that was
almost behind Marian.   People in her rank
of life—women more especially—have a
knack of getting, if possible, out of the
field of vision of those who are speaking to
them.   They do it so religiously that I am
inclined to think they labour under the
impression that it is a point of politeness.

It was really a relief to Marian, who had
not to look straight at that grave carved-
looking face, which reminded her of the
big heads outside some walking-stick shops
—very hard fixed faces, without much
expression.   At the same time she could
watch Mrs. Warner out of the corners of
her eyes unobserved, and see what effect her
words were having upon her.

So, with some hesitation and difficulty,
Marian began her story.   She did not
mention names or places, but she told the
whole story of her life and of the shame
which had befallen her sister.   And then
she told Mrs. Warner—a little more de-
cidedly and distinctly—that she intended to
seek for her sister until she found her.

When she came to the part about Alice,
she saw that Mrs. Warner was making
very peculiar grimaces.   She was screwing

up her hard, uncomely features in a way that reminded one irresistibly of a nut-cracker with a very obdurate nut in its jaws; and then she began to fidget with the tray, to push the dish and plate on it, to move the jug—finally, to twitch the tray-cloth. And when she got as far as that, she fairly broke down, and began to cry, wiping her eyes with the tray-cloth. The contortions which Marian had begun to fear were signs of horror and anger were merely the con-vulsions of a very dry face that had some difficulty in crying because it had not been used to it for such a long time.

This outburst, as may be imagined, took Marian by surprise, and I think she began to cry again, too, for a little while.

Presently, with a great many gulps and peculiar noises, which it is conjectured were sobs rather startled to find themselves in such an apparently uncongenial bosom, Mrs. Warner rose and left the room. Marian heard her go upstairs to her own bedroom. Then came the lugging of a heavy box across the floor; and then down came Mrs. Warner with a faded little sampler. Without a word, she thrust it into Marian's hand.

Marian looked at it, and read—

"JEAN MARY WARNER,"

with the date of her birth. It was Mrs. Warner's daughter.

Marian understood all the story.

"Eh, lassie, the one of all my bairns that I reared; and it a'maist mak's me wish she'd just deed like a' the rest. Eh, my lassie, my lassie!"

Then these two women sat down side by side and comforted each other, for a common sorrow brought them together.

Mrs. Warner related her sad history to Marian in her turn. It was the old, old story—the old sad, bad, wicked story! A pretty face, and an ill-assorted attachment, and then the disappearance of the girl.

Marian tried to console the mother with the hope that after all her daughter was married — that it was only a runaway match.

"Nay, nay! I canna believe that my lassie would ha'e forgot her auld mither that fashion if it had been sae. Ye'll no think that, surely. Besides, there's just ae thing mair."

And then she told Marian that she had

received a letter—or rather an envelope—
containing a lock of a baby's hair, and that
the handwriting was her daughter's, and
the postmark was a London postmark.
" And, eh, Miss Carlyle," said the poor
woman, " ye could no ken the differ between
that wee bit of gowden hair and the lock I
had cut from my daughter's head when she
was a tiny bairn ! "

Marian's object in confiding her story
to Mrs. Warner was to account for her
absence of an evening. She had been
afraid the stern, prim old Scotchwoman
might be prone to think hardly, and would
perhaps make a disturbance about her late
hours. But there was no fear of that
now. Mrs. Warner could feel for her, and
even proposed, kind old soul, to accompany
Marian in her search, because her age
would be some protection to her. But
Marian declined the kind offer.

" There's one, Mrs. Warner, that would
go anywhere for me, by whose side I would
not fear any danger, and he made me the
same offer, but I refused it. For if there's
any one with me, it may scare her away,
poor thing; but I'm hoping, if she ever
sees me alone, looking for her and longing

for her, she won't be able to help running to me and kissing me. And if I can only get her to my heart, I'm thinking she'll never, never want to go away again."

The woman felt Marian was right, so she folded up her poor faded relic, and put it in the bosom of her gown, and then for the first time in her life she kissed Marian; and finally took up the supper tray and disappeared.

Thus was one of Marian's difficulties overcome. Her next task was to tell the Rev. Augustus Rudgeworth.

He visited the school next day, so Marian asked him if he were very busy that morning.

"Not more than usual, Miss Carlyle. In fact, less than usual, for there's less sickness about."

"I'm glad to hear it, sir, for the poor people have had a sore time of it. But if you're not going away till after school, I should like to speak with you particularly, if you wouldn't mind waiting after the children are gone."

"With the greatest pleasure, Miss Carlyle. At least, no! I'm not quite so sure of that, for I'm afraid you're going to tell me that you're going to leave us."

"No, it is not that, Mr. Rudgeworth. On the contrary, I think you will have me here as a fixture—that is, if you choose."

"Choose? We're only too fortunate in getting you."

The Rev. Augustus Rudgeworth goes into the play-yard, and sits down on the low wall that surrounds it and thinks.

He wonders how it is that Marian's intended marriage is put a stop to. He thinks the man must be behaving very badly. "A man might be very happy with such a woman—so clever, such a manager. She and her husband, supposing he had had a university education, might open a school, and make it answer uncommonly well."

You see, the Rev. Augustus is almost falling into a meditation as to the advisability of his proposing to Marian himself. In fact, he is only restrained by the suspicion that if he were to marry, the interest which so many of his female parishioners take in him might be seriously diminished, if not altogether destroyed.

Young parsons will dream these dreams, and be scared from the altar by no more powerful arguments than his.

Presently the hum in the school suddenly breaks into a clamour, and in another minute the youngsters come rushing down the steep wooden stairs like so many small thunderstorms, and then disperse, running, and shouting, and pushing in the greatest possible glee at having done with school for an hour or so.

When the last urchin has gone, the curate goes up to the schoolroom, where Marian is walking up and down nervously.

It is some little time before she speaks, for she finds great difficulty in telling him what she wishes him to know.

He listens attentively, shaking his head sadly when she tells him about poor Alice. At last she announces to him her intention of finding her sister.

"I must work during the day to get my living; and in the evening—all night if I think it will be of use—I shall seek my sister through the length and breadth of London, and I *will* find her. Why I tell you this is, that you may decide, sir, whether you think, under such circumstances, you can continue to employ me here. I know that I shall be misunderstood and misrepresented, but I am determined to find her, cost what it may. If I can get no other means of a livelihood, I must do needlework."

"Miss Carlyle," says the curate, taking her by the hand—and somehow all the ludicrous about him fades away as he does it—"I respect your brave spirit. I pray you may succeed. I can see no reason in such noble devotion to duty why we should seek other aid than yours. On the other hand, it seems to me a further proof of your fitness and of your conscientious discharge of your duties. I am glad you will still work with us, and I feel proud indeed to be associated with you in your labours. Heaven speed your quest!"

He shakes her hand and bows very low—an act of quite involuntary homage—as he takes his leave. A little while ago he was thinking he would condescend to marry this girl. Now he wishes it were his fortune to be worthy of aspiring to it.

"He's a lucky fellow whoever he is that she's going to marry," says the Reverend Augustus Rudgeworth. And he is right!

CHAPTER XI.

CORMACK'S COMING TRIUMPH.

EVERYTHING had been prepared at Wheal Cormack for the great occasion when the engine was to be put to work. But a sudden blight falls on the venture.

Such sudden blights are not uncommon in mining speculations. Of the lotteries in this world, mining is the most uncertain, and, I think, taken altogether, the most unsatisfactory. It is the fashion to speak of the miner as one who gropes in the dark. But the figure does not half convey the real difficulties he has to encounter. Put a man in a dark room, and let him grope about there for a walking-stick, let us say. He goes round and round, or across and across the space until he happens to hit upon the place where his stick is. There is nothing to conceal it from him. But the miner's groping for ore is much more limited. He does not grope in air. He has to find what he wants through stone which it is infinite labour to cut. He may be so near the object of his desires, that only an inch separates him from it; but it is an inch of solid granite. I should like to have the magical power for just one minute to see as in a mirror all the mines that are being driven underground. In how many of them we should see the sturdy, eager miners tearing their way into the bowels of the rock— where all is barren—with a great treasure of the coveted metal within a few feet of their working place.

I believe Henry Cormack would have given a considerable sum for such a glimpse into the internal arrangements of the earth.

For Captain Tregenna has been over to see him, and he reports that the new shaft is sunk several fathoms below the place where they hoped to cut into the lode; but there is not a sign of ore anywhere.

" Keep on sinking, cap'n ! " says Henry Cormack.

" I'm thinking it would be best to drive a level," says the other.

" Do anything you like, only cut the lode before we put the engine to work, or we shall never get East Wheal Cormack floated."

" E'es, sure, 'tis of that I'm thinking," says the captain. " Maybe 'twould be best for to put off the engine a bit."

He says this with evident reluctance; nor is Cormack less desirous than he is of getting the engine up.

" Well, you must try a bit longer, cap'n, and see what you can do."

So the captain goes back to mine ; but he returns in the course of a few days to Polvrehan with a longer face than ever. And no wonder ! for the rich lode which they had been pursuing in the old level has stopped suddenly. It is completely lost !

" The ground was looking so keenly to the la'ast, and now there's neer a bit o' gossan, nor so much 's a scrap of mundick.* She've a-gone so clean as ef you'd a-took mun out with a la'adle ! "

This is bad news indeed. It is evident that during some tremendous volcanic convulsion the crust of the earth containing the vein of metal had been upheaved until it cracked and fell back, but of course did not join exactly. These extraordinary cleavages and derangements of strata are the

* Gossan is the " country," or ground, enclosing the lode. Mundick is iron or arsenical pyrites.

scourge of the miner. Sometimes the variation is very slight, and a little exploring soon brings the men on the right track again. But sometimes they entirely baffle sagacity and experience, and unfortunately the shift of the lode at Wheal Cormack came under the last head.

Captain Tregenna is a shrewd miner, fortunately for Cormack. He has a large quantity of ore on the mine, which he would not send to the " ticketings "—as the sales of the ore are called—for fear of a glut. He will be able for some time, therefore, to keep up the supply, and so conceal to some extent the want of success. There is always an amount of loyalty among the miners which induces them to keep up appearances for the mine they are employed on; so the secret does not ooze out, and nobody outside the concern knows that Wheal Cormack, from being a prosperous venture has suddenly in one minute become a blank.

But there has for a long time been considerable talk in the neighbourhood about the great dinner there was to be when the new engine was put to work.

People know that the engine-house and

stack are built, and that the engine is
ready, too. Cormack sees this difficulty,
and overcomes it in a masterly manner. He
gets the architect to report that the stack
is unsafe, and the engine-house not built
according to plan. He in the meantime
makes a quiet arrangement with the builder.
So the stack and engine-house have to be
pulled down and rebuilt; and as that is an
operation which takes time, he calculates
that they will be able to prosecute their
search for the missing lode in all directions,
and recover it before the festivities.

Luckily for Cormack, James Trefusis is
in no hurry now to obtain possession of
Polvrehan. Even in his misfortunes this
rogue seems favoured by fortune.

When Marian once more broke off their
engagement, poor James felt that there was
little hope of its renewal—at all events, for
a long time. He would not show her how
deeply he felt it, so he determined to creep
away out of sight somewhere. He prevailed
on Charlie Crawhall to go to the South of
France with him. And it was lucky for
him that Charlie did go, for they had not
been on the Continent long before James

was laid up with a severe fever, and only escaped death by a little.

While he is slowly recovering, loitering about the sunny little French village, he thinks nothing more of Polvrehan; and as he has left no instructions with Mr. Totting, his lawyer, that gentleman does not press Henry Cormack to deliver up possession; and he, having urgent reasons for still remaining on the spot, does not evince the slightest desire to vacate the house.

Meanwhile, Captain Tregenna and his corps are working for their lives to hit off the lode again. But it seems to have gone down—it is a dip, and they must sink many fathoms, so the Captain fears, before there is any chance of their seeing ore again.

The house and stack have been pulled down, and are being rebuilt. They are not being a bit better built now than they were before, and they are built of the same materials; so that, on the whole, I take it the architect's condemnation of the old buildings has not conduced to any very great advantage or improvement.

Nearly a twelvemonth passes in this way.

Very slowly it passes over the head of the poor invalid down in the sunny South of France. He is not allowed to be quite unmolested in his peaceful retreat. The English Government, which refused so steadily to take any notice of his invention when he offered it originally, has taken a great fancy to it now that it comes as a foreign invention. "The Secretary of State for War directs" innumerable people, whose signatures are invariably illegible, and whose English is not always faultless, to request that Mr. Trefusis will put himself into communication with the Ordnance Committee, in order that his gun—in the official communications this part is invariably so worded as to mean, grammatically speaking, the Secretary of State's gun—may be tested and examined, with a view to its adoption in the British army.

James, not caring to trouble himself about the matter, does not reply, and, accordingly, a member of the Civil Service is despatched to the South of France, for the special purpose of communicating with Mr. Trefusis on the matters alluded to "in communications from this office, dated etc., etc."

The gentleman to whom this delicate mission is entrusted turns out to be no other than James's old friend—or rather acquaintance, for the terms they were on were those of opponents rather than friends —Mr. Ledbitter. He entirely forgets ever having seen James, or even having heard his name. But separated, as he is, from the depressing influence of the official rabbit-warren in Pall Mall, he is a pleasant enough gentleman, and performs his mission in a very polite and businesslike manner.

He is very sorry to see that Mr. Trefusis is suffering from ill-health, and suggests that he had better return to England for advice. He could then communicate with the Secretary of State about the gun. Finding James not to be caught in this way, he appeals to his patriotism with as little success. James can't help telling him that a little more patriotism among the officials at the office would have saved all this trouble, and that his own patriotism got a fatal chill in the Pall Mall passages. Mr. Ledbitter is very sorry, and says, quite unconscious that he is laying the rod on his own back, that some of the fellows are inattentive, and don't take any interest in their business; and then he branches off into a scheme for improving the Civil Service generally, and his own office in particular. You will always find Government clerks pleasant and instructive company, for they can always be induced, without the least trouble, to discuss the prospects of the service, and the amelioration of their own condition. In a good many instances, you will find it advisable to restrict them to this subject, as they are not entertaining on other topics.

The twelvemonth passes rather slowly for Captain Cormack, who waits day after day for news from the Bal, but only gets the same intelligence—anything but cheerful intelligence—that the lode has not yet been cut in either of the shafts. And this goes on for ten or eleven months.

At last, however, the Captain comes in with a more hopeful story. He produces a stone of ore from the new shaft. Cormack is suspicious for a little while, and thinks the Captain is tricking him with an old specimen, but Tregenna denies the charge strenuously. It is time, he urges, to hurry on the rebuilding of the engine-house and stack. So Cormack wakes up the builder, and the edifice is run up rapidly. And by this time the roof is on, the lode has been cut in the new shaft at a very low level, and has been hit off again, thanks to the indications found in the new cutting, in the old shaft.

So Wheal Cormack is getting into full swing again, and the invitations to the great feast when the new engine is to be put to work, are beginning to fly about. There is to be a dance and a large tea for the Bal maidens, and endless supplies of beef and cider for the men. A tent is to be erected in front of the " Count House," and long tables will be erected in it on tressels, and the adventurers and all the people connected with mining in the neighbourhood (neighbourhood meaning, in this county, where there was no railway as yet, a very large area indeed) are asked to the dinner. Captain Cormack is to take the chair; and there is to be an endless supply of champagne, without which no great venture (and, indeed, no important stroke of business) can be concluded.

Captain Tregenna is elated to a tremendous degree at the notion, and Cormack is glad of an opportunity of getting off a lot

of his land for mining purposes, as well as
for the chance of fuddling a lot of men at
the company's cost, until they get ripe to
buy the shares he has to offer.

Henry Cormack surveys his position with
infinite internal satisfaction. By his own
exertions and industry he has raised himself
to a proud and independent position. He
is very well off; and if in this part of the
world a few people knew what he had been
—and some what he still was—if he was
not entirely popular and universally respected in this immediate neighbourhood,
he, at any rate, possessed the means of
going away and living somewhere else.

Naturally enough, he was not a very
stern and unforgiving judge of his own
actions, but he was really sincere in his
belief that, after all, he couldn't have done
anything so very wrong, or surely he never
would have been so prosperous.

The coming dinner will be the first occasion on which he will publicly appear as
the great proprietor and capitalist of the
district, and he looks forward to it eagerly.
Some of the people who will be there have
snubbed and despised him in former times:
it will be his turn now! All of them will

look up to him with admiration and respect. He spends a good deal of time in arranging a very fine speech for the occasion. He goes down to the quiet banks of Rella of an evening, and recites it with great effect. It is a little long—but then, when a man has been waiting all his life to say it, one can hardly complain if it be a trifle lengthy.

He is a very prosperous and a very comfortable man. Conscience does not trouble him; he has generously pardoned all his own little offences, and he feels that he is rewarded for his clemency by the good fortune which waits on his undertakings. He rides over every day to see how the men are getting on with the engine. He is restless and impatient for the hour of his triumph.

" Will the day never come ? "

When does the day ever fail to come, Henry Cormack ? Sooner or later it comes, and sooner or later it will come for you. I don't think you would hurry those workmen so if you knew all. But you do not-- and it's lucky for you.

You picture yourself at the head of that long table in the tent, haranguing the

III.   M

guests. I can picture you there, but the working out of the subject in each case will be different.

What a strange thing Fate is! Some of us look forward with such anxiety to the day which is destined to be the darkest in our life—the day which, could we only foresee, we should wish indefinitely postponed. We wait and wait, and long and worry, and fret for the day, and then when it comes we wish we had never seen it break.

And then what things we set our hearts upon! Take this Cormack, for instance: he is hovering about the head of the long deal table which the workmen are putting up. If he could only have a foreknowledge of what is to be, he would turn away from that spot with a shudder.

"Eh, won't it be bra'ave fun?" asks Tregenna, coming into the tent. "'Twere worth waiting vor this la'ast twelmonth, eh, Cap'n, for if we had'n a waited it would be awver now, whereas now tes to come. Oh, 'twere well worth waitin' a twelmonth for."

"Worth waiting twenty twelvemonths for," said Cormack.

Well, after all, these things are matters of opinion.

CHAPTER XII.

MAJORA CANAMUS.

IN one of the obscurest streets of the obscurest quarter in the obscure town of Boulogne there appeared just about this time a certain Captain and Mrs. Canton. Boulogne is, I believe, rather accustomed to the sudden unannounced arrival of English people who have very little money and very little luggage, and who stay for indefinite periods, seldom going further inland, but spending much time in gazing across the ocean towards where the white cliffs of England might be supposed to be, but where there is only a dim distance discernible.

I trust I shall be pardoned by our lively neighbours for speaking of that pleasant watering-place, Boulogne, as an obscure town. What I mean is—not that the agreeable place is unknown to the world, for it is far-famed; but that there is hanging about the majority of the English inhabitants a certain cloud and dimness, which envelopes the visitor in a complete fog as to the antecedents, the present means, and the future prospects of those with whom he is thrown into company.

Shabby gentility, and an aristocracy which appears to make its living by playing at billiards, divide the society between them; and it was to the aristocracy that Captain Canton belonged. A neater hand with a cue, and a more sure one at a hazard—under certain circumstances—has seldom, I fancy, been seen. When he struck a ball, there was that "click!" which, to a practised ear, proclaims the stroke of a good player; but unfortunately the Captain was nervous in playing with strangers, and used to bungle sadly. He missed the plainest strokes, and never got a break at all. It was really remarkable.

Of course this diffidence wore off after a time; but as it was generally so obstinate as not to disappear until the Captain's opponent felt confident enough to challenge him to play at heavy stakes, this little defect in his nervous system, instead of being disadvantageous, was—quite accidentally, of course—rather in his favour than otherwise.

I must do the Captain the justice of saying that his non-success always seemed to surprise him. After missing some very easy stroke, he never failed to assure his adversary that " he should do better presently ; " though he lost his temper so often when he had repetitions of ill-luck, that an improvement did not seem likely.

When, however, his adversary began to raise the stakes to any considerable amount, the importance of playing well seemed to nerve the Captain for the effort, and not unfrequently the man who had missed the simplest " pot " in the world, made a cannon after four or five angles, and went off with a break that surprised his opponent considerably.

I suppose it was because knowing them so well he felt no diffidence in playing with them, that the markers at the various tables were not to be prevailed upon to wield a cue against the Captain. Indeed, few of the regular settled inhabitants cared to encounter him on the green cloth—possibly for the same reason.

Captain Canton was a very fascinating man. He could talk any one into a game at billiards—or, indeed, into almost anything. The ladies—what a queer, odd lot they were—all of them thought very highly of him. In fact, to use their own words, they considered him a "dangerous dear."

The Captain and his wife—a delicate woman, who suffered from weakness of the eyes—had been living in great style for some time after they came to the Continent; but not long after the failure of Orr's bank in Babel Court, Lombard Street—in fact, as the news reached them, when they were staying at Hombourg—they drew in their horns, and since that time appeared to have some difficulty in doing what appears to be an everlasting effort, if we may judge from one of the emblems selected to signify eternity —namely, making the two ends meet.

I dare say my readers have found little difficulty in identifying Captain Canton with Major Cantlow, and the miserable woman who passed for his wife with Honoria Vorian, the poor, revengeful creature, who found, as revengeful people often do find, that her studied plan of retribution was telling hardest against herself.

When they heard of old Orr's failure and arrest, you may be sure she had no pleasant time of it. Cantlow was a coward and a bully, and he was consequently very brave as far as words went, and with a woman. He taunted his victim with having cheated him, and declared that she knew of the fate impending over her father when she ran away with him. He had no money invested in the bank in reality, but he complained as much as if all the wealth of the Indies had been placed to his credit there, and had disappeared in the general smash.

They had lived at a princely rate when they first came to Hombourg, for the Captain had calculated that he could always make use of Honoria to draw on her father; and he began accordingly putting in motion a very grand scheme for breaking the bank of the gambling table. It was, he believed, an infallible scheme. Like all gamblers, he nursed the hope of inventing such a plan, and he had had ample time to mature his design, for he had never had the requisite funds to put his theory into practice, and so had gone on proving and trying, correcting minor details, and bringing every minute point to the utmost perfection. Now, for

the first time perhaps in his life, he had
the means of putting his theory to the test,
and he determined to give it a full trial.

He lost heavily at first—very heavily
indeed, and even in the face of the belief
that he could always fall back upon Mr.
Orr for supplies, was a little startled at the
heavy set against him. But his theory was
not a rapid scheme of demolition. It was
the result of a calculation of chances, and
would have to be put off until he had
calculated the average run of luck for
many nights. Then he would try his
grand coup!

He played night after night, and for a
time fortune changed, and he began to win
a little; but the fickle goddess did not smile
long. He began to lose as heavily as ever
again.

The old *habitués* of the table soon came
to perceive that he was exploiting a scheme,
and watched him. The other players looked
on with wonder at a man who lost and won
with such equanimity.

" Doubtless a milord Anglais, " said
Adolphe, who was boldly venturing his
louis, whispering to Beniot, who was going
in for five-franc pieces.

"Oh, but yes; and by my faith a rich one!" says his friend.

"This monsieur," says the old Count Balbaisse, whose white moustache has swept that green cloth any time these ten years, "this monsieur has a plan infallible to to break the bank;" and he shrugs his shoulders.

"Ah," says the gray-headed old colonel to whom he confides this, " we have seen so many such, eh?"

"And all equally successful!"

" Yes, by my faith, all."

"This seems to me the same that crazed that poor Cadousalle, who blew out his brains yonder;" and the count tosses one end of his gray moustache over his left shoulder in the direction of a neighbouring hotel.

But Cantlow perseveres with a courage worthy of a better cause, and Honoria figures, to her great delight, at the balls and entertainments. The time for the English has not yet arrived, so she runs no danger of being recognised. And she figures about in all her jewels, and makes half the foreigners in love with her brilliants and her weak eyes.

But one night, as she is in the midst of her gaiety, comes to her the Major, with a pale face and fiery eyes. He clutches her by the wrist, heedless of the fact that she has a meek partner waiting until she buttoned her glove, to conduct her through the pleasant mazes of the waltz. The Major half drags her to a quiet corner, where he takes an English paper from his pocket, and shows her the news of her father's failure and arrest for forgery.

" Good gracious ! Can it be true ? " she says slowly, after a long pause, during which she has read and re-read the paragraph as if she doubted the evidence of her eyes.

" True ! oh, true enough ! Why the deuce didn't I see through his cursed commercial successes and his ostentatious honesty ? "

" I cannot and will not believe it. He may be unfortunate, but I am sure he has done nothing wrong."

" Oh, gammon ! " says the feeling Major. " He's just as big a cheat as the rest, and you knew it, and that's the reason why you ran away with me."

" Sir, you forget yourself ! " says Honoria,

who is conscious that her meek partner is hovering in the neighbourhood, waiting till this jealous Englishman has done scolding his wife for dancing with such a fascinating Adonis.

" Oh, no, I don't. I'm thinking of myself fast enough, and what a deuce of a hole you've let me into. I've spent nearly all the money, and I haven't given my scheme anything like half a trial. Egad, when I said I'd fight it out till the bank broke, I little thought it would be the bank in Babel Court ! "

" What will they do to him if—if it should be true ? " asks Honoria with some difficulty.

" Hang him, I hope."

" Oh, no ! " she gasps, clutching his arm, " not that, surely not that ! Tell me not that ! "

" What a fool you are. I should have thought you would have known they don't hang for forgery now-a-days. Hasn't it been talked over in the family ? I believe it's a little family swindle. You don't suppose I'm going to believe you weren't all in it ! "

Honoria was ready to strike him almost;

but she was obliged to curb her temper, for she wished to learn the worst.

"Will you tell me honestly and civilly what is the extent of punishment that can be awarded in such a case—where—where the person is guilty?"

"Depends on the amount. I suppose he did it for something handsome—you'll know the amount, I dare say—and if it's large, why it will be transportation for life; and"—here the Captain ground his teeth and swore frightfully—"if they hanged him, it would not be a bit less than he deserved!"

So the Major went back to the gaming table, where he lost with less grace than usual; and Honoria returned to the ballroom, where she danced with less grace than usual. And within a day or two they took their departure, and when next we hear of them are domiciled in the shabby lodgings of the shabby street of shabby Boulogne, where we found Captain and Mrs. Canton at the beginning of the chapter.

From the evening when he told her the news of her father's failure and disgrace, the conduct of the Major to Honoria altered entirely. He had become indifferent at Hombourg—at Boulogne he was brutal.

She was left to her own resources entirely. She could have no gaiety; and if she could have had it, would not have cared for it, because her jewels had all gone to pay the Captain's gambling debts. As he intended making a long sojourn in Boulogne, he was extremely scrupulous as to debts of honour.

They had to depend on his skill—perhaps I might use a less pleasant word—for their livelihood, and I must do him the credit of saying that he worked at his profession unceasingly. Few pigeons landed in Boulogne on a flight from the British isles without undergoing a plucking at the hands of the Captain. He was generally the fortunate winner of the first pluckings, for he was of a gentlemanly exterior, and these poor pigeons had as a rule been warned against seedy swindlers only, and so fell into his trap the more readily, especially as he usually told them, in strict confidence, within a few minutes after they had begun to play, that it was very unsafe to take a cue with a stranger in this seaport, as he had found to his cost, etc., etc.—putting his dupe so off his guard that his fleecing was made a certainty.

Unfortunately, nobody can pluck pigeons without leaving a few feathers about, and occasionally, too, permitting a bird to escape half-plucked as a warning to his companions.

So at last the Captain's little game began to be too well known, and business was a little slack.

What sufferings Honoria underwent then were terrible. While he had been pretty successful, he had doled her out a paltry pittance, which she, with the wonderful adaptability of her sex to circumstances, had contrived to make answer all her necessities.

But when his skill began to fail in supplying him with money, he cut off her poor allowance altogether. She must get money how she could; she might write to her father or her mother—or her husband—for it. He was obliged to have a little cash about him—was obliged to keep a stock-in-trade—to dine and smoke and drink like a gentleman.

Then the struggle became hard indeed for Honoria. At first she tried to get out of her difficulty by borrowing of the landlady, and telling her to ask the Captain for the money when he came in. But the Captain only said very politely, "Oh, if madame borrows, madame must pay;" so she did not get much by that move.

At last she was reduced, in order to get a few francs to pay for her dinner, to use the miserable accomplishments with which her education had been adorned as a girl. She sold little shell-covered models to the shops—paintings of flowers and bits of fancy work—earning just enough to give her a few pence profit beyond the cost of the materials.

So she struggled on for a time.

At last there came to Boulogne a wealthy young Englishman, the son of a prosperous manufacturer, who gave him a full purse and leave to travel. With this young fellow the Captain speedily struck up a close and warm acquaintance. At first the young fellow was so generous, and fond of giving dinners to his new friend, so delighted to have a guide and philosopher at any price, that the Captain had no need to pluck him.

But however generous a man may be, he

grows rather tired of giving dinners and fêtes without any invitation in return.

So at last the Captain, being almost taunted with his want of hospitality by his new friend, invited him to a dinner ; and he determined after dinner to invite the young fellow to play, and then and there to bleed him to the best of his power.

But the lad had been at the University a term or two, and had matriculated in billiards there, and was not an easy prey. The Captain had to play his best, and to exercise his most cunning craft in order to get any advantage of his opponent.

Unfortunately, he was driven to try, as a last resource, a little sharp practice, which was detected. Sharp words ensued ; and the quarrel at last waxed so warm that the young manufacturer advanced to the Captain with his fists doubled, promising him a sound thrashing.

The Captain, or rather—to paint him in his true colours—Major Cantlow, was a coward. When he saw his opponent coming at him, he turned deadly pale, sprang back, and, just as the lad was about to strike him, felled him with a clubbed cue, and then ran from the place.

This happened abroad, you remember, and there was only one course to be adopted there under such circumstances. A friend of the young Englishman called at Cantlow's lodgings next morning to appoint a hostile meeting.

But there was no Cantlow to be found!

Honoria had heard him come in the night before—had heard him moving about in the sitting-room for some time—had heard him go downstairs and leave the house. Since then she knew nothing of him.

Before long it was too apparent that this cur had fled—had run away, and left this most unhappy of women alone and penniless.

Then came for her the very bitterest struggle of all.

With burning tears, with agony and shame insupportable, she wrote a letter to her husband, confessing her fault, asking pardon, and imploring relief. It was the last and only resource that was left for her; and it was not until she was driven to it by the direst necessity that she posted the letter.

Then she sat down, and waited to see what her fate was to be.

III.   N

CHAPTER XIII.

GOING HOME.

WHEN Henry Vorian received his wife's letter, he said nothing to Lord and Lady Lacquoigne, but went straight off to Mrs. Orr.

He had not much difficulty in finding her. She had, as we know, saved something out of the wreck, and was now living in a pretty public retirement under the assumed character of a deeply-wronged woman. I dare say the greater part of the world thought her so; for the greater part of the world is ready enough, as a rule, to take one for what one represents oneself to be. But accepting her definition of her position, it quietly let her drop, nevertheless. She was an injured woman in more senses than one; she had lost her wealth and position, and that is an injury in the eyes of society that nothing can atone for. Pitied, but passed by, Mrs. Orr was bewailing her fate in a small cottage near Richmond.

Thither, accordingly, Henry Vorian made his way with Honoria's letter.

At first he was refused admittance, for Mrs. Orr supposed he had come to claim his child, to which she was much attached as the last relic of the daughter she had really loved. Henry pencilled the reason of his wish to see her on the back of his card, and sent it up to her. He was at once ushered in.

Mrs. Orr was dressed in something as nearly like a widow's suit of weeds as possible; in fact she had everything on but the cap, which I suppose was hardly the correct thing to wear while her husband was alive. It was a sort of protest—as if she said, "I ought to be a widow, and should be if unfortunately I had not a husband who still dares to exist."

Henry Vorian did not say much to this strange woman, with her tenderness for her child and her sternness to her husband. He handed her the letter.

She burst into tears at the sight of the well-known angular handwriting. How well she remembered Honoria's acquiring that elegant Italian hand—an accomplishment she almost envied her. When the daughter of the house could write like that, you may depend upon it all the invitation notes and other cartels demanded by Society were penned by her, and she had ample employment. Mrs. Orr had reason to remember that hand, though not altogether from the number of fond and affectionate letters her child had written to her.

With much sobbing and a great deal of grief, which was, I believe, not the less real and deep because it was vulgar and noisy, Mrs. Orr read Honoria's wild and rambling epistle through once or twice. She could not quite understand it the first time, owing partly to her own state of perplexity, partly to her daughter's incoherency. When she had at last finished the perusal, she turned to Henry.

"What do you intend to do?"

"What do you advise?"

"You will take her back and forgive her?"

"Never! That I am determined on."

"Then why — why did you come to me?"

"I thought you might wish to assist her.

I did not need advice from you as to my own course. Had I needed advice on that, I should have sought it of my father and mother."

"Oh, they'd give you hard enough advice of course. But there—I didn't mean to say anything rude. Forgive me—and give me your advice."

"The best thing you can do is to send her some money. She says she is starving!"

"Poor dear—poor dear! And she used to every luxury—at least while she was with us."

"She was not starved while at my house, madam, though I did not give such sumptuous dinners as Mr. Orr."

"There—there, I didn't mean to offend you. Oh, dear—oh, dear, what am I to do? I should like to have my child here with me, but how is it to be done?"

With all her vulgarity, Mrs. Orr was an artful and very persuasive woman. She found it would be to her advantage to conciliate Henry, and she took all trouble to do so. She cajoled and lamented, she implored and entreated, and succeeded at last in enlisting his sympathy.

Henry Vorian was not, as the reader of this story, I hope, knows, a very bad man—certainly not a cruel one. He softened somewhat at the picture Mrs. Orr drew of the abject distress of the woman who had been in name at least a wife to him. Possibly the face which he had seen and believed almost to be the face of a ghost, softened him a little, too.

The end was that he actually promised Mrs. Orr to go over and fetch Honoria from Boulogne, and bring her to her mother. It would have been a foolish—nay, a fatal mistake in the eye of his lawyer, but it never occurred to Henry to consult Mr. Scrooby on the subject.

I don't think, to do her justice, Mrs. Orr knew that by such an act Henry was compromising his case. She was only most anxious to recover her child, and saw in him her sole chance of doing so.

It was arranged that Mrs. Orr should write to Honoria and send her some money at once, and that in the letter containing it she should prepare her for Henry's arrival, and explain to her clearly his purpose in so doing.

" Impress upon her that my thus rescuing her from want and impending disgrace is the last and utmost act of consideration or pardon she is to expect from me."

Mrs. Orr promised — and performed. Honoria was warned of her husband's intention to fetch her from Boulogne, and hand her over to her mother—"who would be only too happy amid her wrongs and miseries to welcome back her dearest child. She could forgive and forget the past, though others could not and would not— not even the man who had married her simply for her money." You see, she said nothing about the parents who sold her for a title.

Honoria was in a terrible state of per- turbation at the news of her husband's intention to fetch her. She could not but feel that his doing thus much was far more than she deserved, and she felt deeply grateful. But still she dreaded the meeting.

There was in reality little to dread. He came to her with a cold reserve, as if he had been almost a stranger, and it chilled and deadened the warm feelings of gratitude she would fain have expressed.

They met as if they were the most casual and careless of acquaintance.

The morning of the day on which they were to set sail for England dawned dark and louring. A long bank of leaden clouds obscured the horizon, and straggling detachments of ominous-looking vapours hurried past overhead. The sea was of the same dull hue as the sky, whitening more and more with ragged white foam edges—like grinning teeth—as the rack thickened overhead. For from the long low bank of cloud there presently began to spread a gloomy canopy that filled the heavens with a sombre lurid twilight.

Whiter grew the sea, and louder and angrier was its voice, as it flung its long waves on the echoing shore.

There were no fishing boats out. The sailors looked to windward, and shook their heads when you asked why they did not put out.

Many of the passengers who were to go by the steamer cried off; for it was clearly going to be very ugly weather indeed.

With a terrible recollection of their honeymoon tour, Henry remembered that his wife suffered much in the smoothest sea. He felt it would be almost brutal to ask her to face such a storm as was coming.

He told her of his intention to wait until the storm had passed—that they should probably sail the next day, and that in the meantime, as she had given up her lodgings, he would take rooms for her at his hotel. She was very grateful for the consideration. But he checked at once any expression of her feeling by his coldness. He felt that it was necessary to assume a stern and un-yielding position towards her, lest she should be induced to hope that he might relent and forgive her. That was out of the question.

The day did not belie the promise of the morning. The packet put out twice, and was twice compelled to put back. The third time she managed to make her way out, and stood away for England. There were many anxious eyes fixed on her that watched her until the thick curtain of rain, which presently descended, shut her from their sight. She had a fearfully rough passage, and was very late, but she reached her destination at last in safety.

The storm came down heavily on the French coast. First of all came the thick darkness of the rain, to be presently gashed and seamed by vivid flashes of blue lightning, followed by peals of thunder that made the whole town tremble.

It was a terrible and yet a grand sight. Henry Vorian spent the evening in watching it. He did not care to go to his hotel till late, so he braved the pitiless beating of the rain, and with a few courageous spirits, and those whose duty it was to do so, he stood on the pier and watched the conflict of the elements.

Night came on early, so thick was the gloom. And still the storm raged and roared. At last, wearied out, Henry Vorian sought his hotel.

The lady, he was told, had been greatly terrified by the thunder and lightning, and had gone to bed some hours ago. He was not sorry for it, for he was saved the pain of an interview. He sat and smoked a cigar, and then retired to rest. As she showed him the way to his room, the chambermaid pointed out to him the room where madame slept. She was, said the chambermaid, almost asleep when she looked in there, but "elle a souffert beaucoup," said the kind little creature; adding, that she did not wonder, for such an awful tempest had not been known for years.

Henry was very weary. He got into bed as rapidly as he could, and was soon in that half-conscious state bordering on actual sleep when we mingle realities with our visions.

In this drowsiness he was still in imagination watching the storm—as he might have done had he been awake, for his bedroom was high up, and looked on the sea, and he had not drawn down the blind. All at once it seemed to him that a flash of lightning and a short but loud clap of thunder came almost simultaneously. Then another! At the second he was wide awake, and sprang up in bed.

A third came. About this there was no mistake. He could see the flash from his window. But it was not lightning, nor was the roar that followed it thunder. Henry Vorian knew what it was. He was soon hurrying on his clothes. But other eyes and ears in the hotel had noted the flash and report, and before he was quite dressed there was a scuffling to and fro in the passages, and the sound of voices.

It was a vessel driving ashore that had fired the signals of distress, and everybody was on the alert at once.

As he hurried by Honoria's door, he saw that it was open, and beheld her pale face peering round. When she saw him, she cried out, "What is it? What does it all mean? Is the place on fire?"

"No! no! Go to bed again. It is a ship in distress, and we're going to see what is to be done—that's all—don't be alarmed."

"You're not going into danger?" she said, half-timidly, half-imploringly.

"What matter if I am? Good night!" and he hurried downstairs, and made his way to the beach.

It was a large three-masted vessel, which appeared to have lost its rudder, and to have had its sails blown to ribbons. It was driving rapidly on shore.

There was no time to be lost, but the noisy and demonstrative Frenchmen were losing as much of it as they could.

Luckily, there was a little knot of Englishmen, some landsmen, some sailors, and they were quietly busying themselves in getting out a boat.

"How many of you can row?" asked one of the sailors, who, from the deference paid to him by the others, was probably a lower officer.

Several of the landsmen volunteered, and the sailor chose out the likeliest-looking to make up the crew. Among those he selected was Henry Vorian.

"Pull steady, in Heaven's name, my men—run her down into the surf, and jump in as quickly as you can—in order—bow first. Now then! Ready! Run her down!" But the sea beat them back, and threw them on the shore, overturning the boat.

They were not to be disheartened, though. Half the crew got in her this time, and had their oars out ready to pull, while the remainder, aided by some of the bystanders, pushed her off.

It was a fierce, sharp struggle; but they managed this time to get her off.

"Steady, lads!   A long stroke, and keep time—put your backs into it, boys!" shouted the old sailor who had taken the helm.

They rowed manfully, though the sea was terribly high, and the boat could hardly be expected to live in it.   Not a word was spoken save by the sailor at the helm, who cheered the rowers on, or cautioned them against rowing wildly.

They were near enough to the ship now to see the people clinging to the rigging, and to distinguish the cries with which the sight of the boat was welcomed.

She was breaking up fast.   Planks and spars were washed by the boat as she struggled up to the vessel, which was just stranding—bumping-on as every fresh sea lifted her further ashore.

"Now, then, steady, lads, steady.   We must take her in very carefully, or we shall be swamped!" said the old sailor.

Just at this moment a floating spar, carried along by a tremendous sea that swept the boat from stem to stern, struck him in the chest and knocked him overboard. The boat, no longer steered to take the seas, swung broadside on. There was a rush to pick up the steersman and take the rudder—and almost at the same moment a monster wave came roaring on and engulfed the boat, full in the sight of the wrecked ship, whence arose a cry of despair and horror at the awful fate which had overtaken those who were coming so gallantly to the rescue.

Only two sailors out of the whole boat's crew reached land.

So perished Henry Vorian!

Of Honoria's distress I need tell you nothing. She was, indeed, half mad with grief, for she felt that she was, to some degree, the cause of his death. It was his consideration for her that had brought him into the peril.

Her distress moved worthy Mr. Gleeson, who, with his wife and family, was returning from a visit to Paris. He was only a grocer, and therefore had no knowledge of the private history of the Vorians. He kindly offered to take charge of the poor lady who had been so suddenly bereaved—

and under such heartrending circumstances. Honoria accepted the offer, and was safe and sound in her mother's cottage, near Richmond, several days before her unfortunate husband's mangled corpse was washed up upon the inhospitable coast.

CHAPTER XIV.

"THE BLACK-FLOWING RIVER."

WEARILY—very wearily, through heat and cold, through wet and dry—had Marian pursued her quest. Undaunted by failure and undeterred by contempt and derision, she held to her purpose with an undying determination. She *would* find her sister.

How often as she paced the streets, looking wistfully into the poor raddled faces that flitted by, how often had she been led to believe some passing figure was like her sister's. And then with what patient resolution had she tracked that form until her opportunity came, and she went up under the flaring gas to look at the face —and find it was not Alice's.

She became well known to the poor ghosts she haunted, herself a ghost. Pale, dishevelled women were half afraid of her, and shrank from her hungry looks. Some of the more hardened called her "Crazy Jane," and she became known to all the strange inhabitants of the night-side of London by that name. But even the most hardened avoided a meeting with her, if possible—they were all superstitious, these poor creatures, whose first fault had been over-faith, and they shrank terrified from the mystery that surrounded Marian.

"By Jove, there goes that woman again!" languid young men about town used to say when they saw that veiled and shawled figure glide by. They were not capable of deep wonder, or strong enough mentally to try and unravel the secret of that haunting form. They used to solve the mystery with "a midnight meeting party, or something of that sort, you know." Which, after all, was an intellectual effort.

Sometimes she was noticed by some young fellow with a better brain or a warmer heart—some fine lad just passing for a time through the ghastly gas-lit world of midnight, as too many noble natures do, and I trust escape unharmed. It is not their fault so much as the fault of society, that talks glibly about young men "seeing

life." Seeing life! seeing death in life—
seeing how much like corpses live men
and women can be. Some of these better
natures, fallen upon evil times and places,
would be seized with the chivalrous notion
of learning all about this strange cloaked
figure. And then they gave Marian much
trouble — they terrified her, for she could
hardly be expected to know their motives
were honest, finding them where she did.
She was less molested by the regular
denizens of midnight.

The police knew her by sight pretty well,
and affected a complete knowledge of her.
When questioned about her, they looked
sagacious, and said, "Oh, yes, they knowed
her, and what her game was. It warn't no
harm; she bought second-hand clothing, and
sold it, and retailed brushes, and combs,
and soap. A Jewess she was—lived down
Houndsditch somewheres."

You see it would never do for the force
to appear ignorant of anything—especially
in the midnight world, over which they
rule as despots, and exercise a ferocious
tyranny, which quiet citizens who go to bed
at regular hours would hardly believe them
capable of. In the central region of mid-

night they reign by sheer brute force. " I'll lock you up ! " is the only argument they condescend to use; and woe betide the chance passenger who, seeing them maltreating some poor creature they have in custody, ventures to expostulate. He finds himself in a police cell before he can think, and learns next morning, to his surprise, that he is a constant frequenter of haunts of vice and intoxication, and bosom companion of the prisoner in the dock. If it were not for this fertility of their invention in the matter of evidence, the police would be the stupidest body of men in England. And if darkness has once closed over London, and the gas is lit, the humane chance passenger will have a bad time of it to prove himself innocent. The lives, property, and characters of those who, from choice or necessity, are out in the streets after dark, are entirely in the power of the police—a body of ill-paid and undereducated men, with a strong instinct to support one another's allegations. This may seem severe ; but it is true. A working literary man, especially if he be employed in journalism, is obliged to be about London at all hours, and I have, in my own expe-

rience, seen acts of ferocious brutality on
the part of the police—and too often exercised towards those poor unfortunates, whose
appearance in the inhospitable streets at
such hours should have been a reason for
pity, not cruelty.

It was lucky, therefore, for Marian that
she was looked upon by the force as a
huckster of second-hand wardrobes, and
soaps, and sponges. Her quest was set
down as a search after some absconding
customer who was in her debt; and the
recovery of money for goods supplied being
a perfectly legal course, the constables did
not think of interfering with her.

So Crazy Jane is allowed to go her way
unmolested, and pursues her quest night
after night for many a long wearisome
month. But all in vain !

Day after day she taught at her tiny
school, where the children, and perhaps the
Rev. Augustus Rudgeworth too, noticed that
she had become very tender and solicitous
about the big girls who were just leaving
school to go into business or service. We
know why she took an interest in them.
Those who have looked on the world of
midnight may well be full of pity for these

young creatures sent out alone amid great temptation.

"Teacher" was still very popular with the little people she had to educate. Through them she had come to be known to the fathers and mothers, and they sometimes in their difficulties came to "Teacher" for advice. But all this increased her work; and she was growing thin, and old, and gray, before her time. For instead of getting her natural rest at night, she was pacing the inhospitable miles of gas-lit London, pursuing her quest.

Night after night, until the dawn began to show over the house-tops, she wandered wearily to and fro, seeking the lost one. And then, when the gray light began to broaden, she sought her humble roof, and snatched a few hours of rest, broken by dreams in which she was still journeying after her sister; so that sleep scarcely refreshed her.

At last came the close of autumn. The regular November weather descended on London.

It was a night of thick fog. It had done its best all day to rain through the solid yellow cloud, and had contrived to make the flagstones humid and slimy. The lamps were burning dimly, like the bleared eyes of dissipated monsters that had been up a good many nights running, and were getting rather tired of it. They blinked dismally, as if the fog had got into them and made them sore. It was a nasty, pestilential thing, that fog—a tangible, obtrusive horror. Your hands and face were black with its foul caresses, and the purity of your clean collar perished utterly before you had been out in it a minute.

It made you feel ill, because it made you feel dirty. For just as, when you don't feel very well, the smartening of yourself up and the putting on of your best clothes gives you a feeling and air of convalescence —I have known a bilious attack entirely cured by a clean shirt and a new cravat— so the sense that in spite of all the attention you could pay to your *toilette*, you were, the instant you emerged into that beastly atmosphere, a begrimed and blackened wretch, took all the moral starch out of you, and you became limp and unwholesome.

There was a continual, consistent drizzle, as if it were raining very hard indeed on the top of the fog, but the drops could only filter and crawl slowly through that dense medium. It choked you. You longed to gasp, but knew that to do so was merely to swallow the abomination wholesale.

There was a dreadful silence about it. The elastic nature of the air seemed gone. If any one had fired a cannon in the next street, the report would only have come to you as a dull thud, as if some body were shutting a front door ten paces off. All the roar and rattle of the traffic died into a dull rumble, as the various vehicles, magnified into colossal machines, darkened upon you suddenly through the gloom, and then faded away.

And how cold it was! Not the sharp, biting cold of a frosty, windy day, when the northeaster gives you a rubbing down that sets you a-glow again; but the crawling, damp chill that laps you round slowly in its folds, like a horrible snake, freezing the marrow in your bones, and numbing the blood in your veins.

It had been bad enough all day, but the night made it twenty times worse. The thick darkness was made so appreciable by the red blots which stood for lamps. There were no glittering lines of gas. You saw about three red fungoid blotches, differing widely in intensity. As you came near the brightest—or, better, the least dark, it developed into something not unfamiliar—an object between the gas-lamp of ordinary life and the unsnuffed dip. Then it rapidly died out, and the next blot assumed its shape—another small gloomily glowing point dawning on you at the same time. You never got more than the ghosts of three lamps into your field of sight at once. Even the gay, variegated globes at the chemist's were obscured into leprous blotches and diseased flushes, suggestive of blood, jaundice, verdigris, and blue-mould.

But the worst place of all, the part of London where the fog seemed to reign without dispute—was the river.

Inky black and sluggish, a very Lethe, the dark, seemingly motionless, flood spread away beneath you as you looked over the bridges. No reflected lights danced on its bosom. Gleaming window and glaring lamp were blotted out.

What a night for a suicide! What a night for some poor creature, wearied out of existence, to take that fatal plunge which now—with that dim, vapour-wrapt deep beneath—would seem like a leap into futurity !

And such a poor wretch there was upon Waterloo Bridge that night. The sordid, dripping bundle of rags in one of the recesses was a woman, cowered on the dank stones, passing through the agony of dissolution, suffering the pangs of separation, without which there is no death, wilful or natural. For the unhappy being who attemps violently to wrench himself from life, goes through all the long farewells, the regrets, the remorses, the sorrows, which we are prone to believe are gathered in review around the death-bed only. While the hand is raising the hasty knife, while the hurried foot is climbing the parapet, while the trembling finger is drawing the trigger, be sure that inexorable memory reveals at a glance the panorama of the past, and condenses hours of grief into the death-spasm of an instant.

Tottering painfully—groping as if smitten with blindness—possibly smitten with the blindness of bitter tears—the miserable woman rises from the hard flagstones and leans over the chilly, dripping parapet. Darkness below—the lapping of the water at the buttresses of the bridge is almost inaudible—so dull and heavy is the atmosphere. The broad, silent stream seems so deep and inscrutable that the poor heart almost dares to hope it might suck one unnoticed corpse into its inky jaws, out of the sight even of Heaven, to utter oblivion and complete annihilation.

She bends backwards for one moment to listen. It is all so very quiet. The fog hushes all. No fear of the plunge being heard!

Then she mounts the stone seat with uncertain steps, and planting one foot on the parapet, looks up—one long, last appealing look towards heaven.

*　　　*　　　*　　　*

" It is a wretched night to welcome one back to Old England," thought James Trefusis, as he came away shivering from the railway station, after a long and stormy voyage across the Bay of Biscay.

He has been tormented into returning home by the authorities at the Ordnance Office, now the Ordnance Office no longer, but budding afresh—with all its old imperfections considerably strengthened by transplanting—under a new name. The authorities have been just as persistent in worrying him for the Trefusis gun as they had formerly been in declining to give it a trial. But when they had let loose Mr. Ledbitter at him twice, and wrote, threatening a third infliction, James gave in, and made up his mind to come back to England. He is quite well and strong now, so the rough passage does him no harm, nor does he care much for the peculiarly English weather which welcomes him back to his native land.

" I'll walk instead of taking a hansom," says he to himself, " and see if I can't stir up my circulation. I'm regularly damped through with the fog, and washed out with the journey."

So he strides out of the station.

* * * *

It is hardly to be wondered at that Marian in the gloom and uncertainty of such a night as this should pursue several vain shadows; and she has been so intent upon the figure she fondly believed to be Alice's in each case, that she has wandered she scarcely knows whither. At last she finds herself by the river side, and can see looming dark through the fog on her left a bridge. In answer to her inquiries, a man, who is smoking a pipe on board a lighter, moored alongside of the wharf to which she has come astray, tells her it is Waterloo Bridge.

The place seems so strange to her that she becomes impressed with the idea that she must be somewhere on the Surrey side of the water. She is so strongly impressed with this notion that she makes her way at once towards the bridge with the intention of crossing it.

It is more bitterly cold than ever on the bridge. She wraps her shawl closely round her and hurries across. As she reaches the middle arch, and is gliding hastily, noiselessly past it, she sees the flutter of a dress. She looks up and sees a woman standing on the parapet, just about to leap into the river.

In an instant she has sprung to her, caught her round the waist, and dragged her back. The poor wretch is weak, but struggles desperately.

"Let me go! Let me go!"

At that voice Marian is seized with a fearful faintness. There is a lamp close by. She staggers to it, half carrying, half dragging the intended suicide with her.

"Alice! Alice! at last!" is the great cry that breaks from her as the feeble rays fall upon the pale, worn features before her.

"You, Marian? Oh, let me go, then! Let me go!"

And the unhappy girl struggles madly, and almost breaks away from the encircling arms.

Marian feels her strength failing. "Together, then, Alice," she gasps, for she feels she cannot hold the other back much longer.

But just at this moment a violent fit of coughing deprives Alice of all power of resistance. She becomes a dead weight in the arms of Marian, who, too weak to sustain her, sinks on the pavement, holding her sister's head on her lap, and wiping away the blood-tinged foam that soon gathers on her lips.

Can any one tell where a London crowd comes from? In another minute Marian looks up, and find herself surrounded by curious spectators. There is a policeman among them.

"Drunk again, eh? And *you* ain't much better," is his feeling remark.

But before he has time to take any further steps to assert his position, he is thrust aside by a gentleman who has just come up.

It is James Trefusis, walking—how providentially!—from the station. He recognises Marian, and sees all at a glance.

"Go and fetch a cab," he says to a bystander, and he says it with such an air of authority that the man runs off at once, and is back with the vehicle before the constable has had time to collect his rudely scattered senses.

As soon as the cab arrives, James lifts Alice into it, and then assists Marian in.

"I say, who are you?" the policeman has just recovered enough self-possession to inquire. "You're interfering with the police in the execution of their duty. If you don't take care, I'll lock you up."

"Stand back," says James angrily, preparing to mount the box. "Drive on, cabman."

"I'll take yer number, and summons you

if you do," says the constable ; and the cab-man, knowing the power of the police, does not dare to drive on.

The cabman thus failing him, James is compelled to adopt different tactics. He gets down from the box and approaches the policeman.

"Don't you see, we don't want any dis-turbance ? The young woman is mad, and has escaped from the asylum, and the nurse and myself have been looking for her, and have only just found her." Here some-thing, an object held between James's thumb and forefinger, touches the inside of the policeman's Berlin glove. That func-tionary, whose sense of touch is very acute —so acute that he is quite sure, in spite of the intervention of the thick glove, that the object is half-a-crown, and not a florin— says immediately, with a sudden advent of intelligence, "Ah, yes. I guessed as much. It's all right, sir. You can drive on, cabby. Good night, sir."

So the cab drives off, and the crowd dis-perses, much edified, no doubt, by the manner in which individual constables administer the law.

And the night comes down darker and

denser, and all through it Marian, kneeling by the bed, watches her sister—still with that strange feeling, which she cannot get rid of, that Alice is very much older than she.

James had seen them to the door, and waited until they were safely in charge of Mrs. Warner, whose stony gray eyes were over-running with tears. Then James imprinted one kiss on Marian's thin wasted hand, and left the women together.

CHAPTER XV.

SEEKING VENGEANCE.

THE day after the finding of Alice, James Trefusis comes, by the invitation of Mrs. Warner, to see Marian and inquire after her sister. And from that day he becomes a pretty constant visitor, for he is not in the way, and will run on any errands, and becomes, in fact, that most useful compound, half nurse, half porter, which only a strong man, with a big heart full of love, can be.

For many days they move about the house with the hushed step which is so terribly significant of death's vicinage. Marian and Mrs. Warner, however, will not acknowledge the grim neighbour any further. They fight him resolutely. Sleep and rest they despise—watching hourly, almost momentarily, by the bedside, anticipating every want, and alleviating every throe, for Alice is terribly ill. She lies propped with pillows, scarcely conscious—a mere skeleton, with a great red spot on each sunken cheek, and all the veins starting and swelling under the pale clammy skin.

They send for a doctor. He is a clever man; but he shakes his head when he sees his patient, and there comes into his face that expression which those who have learnt by many sick-beds to study the countenances of doctors cannot mistake. But he does not despair—that is a thing he never dreams of. He feels the struggle is a little unequal, and that the enemy has had a long start of him; but that only makes him go into the contest with the greater determination.

In a wonderfully short time, considering the case, he has strengthened and restored his patient considerably; but a close observer might have noted that the expression I have spoken of had not passed away. Marian, however, and Mrs. Warner have grown quite hopeful. James shares their pleasure at Alice's probable recovery. And now that the crisis seems past, James Trefusis speaks to Marian once more.

"My own, she is found now, and the trials and troubles are all past. Be my wife now, Marian."

"I must never leave her, James."

"Do you think I could ask you?"

"No, James, no! But it must not be— it cannot be. What wife would they call me, bringing you no dowry but shame?"

"No, no, Marian. They cannot say it. It would be a lie."

"It would be too true. And she can never really be well and strong again, the doctor says, but will require constant attendance. How could I be your wife without neglecting her, or her nurse without neglecting you? I tell you, James dear, it can never be. We must bear our lot as we best may, for it cannot be otherwise."

"Let us be man and wife, Marian, and we'll watch and tend our sister—oh, how lovingly!—down yonder in that quiet Cornish home of ours. It will be fresh life to her to breathe the dear old air again."

"You do not doubt that I love you, James?" asks Marian, coming up to him, putting her hands in his, and looking him frankly in the eyes.

"Never, my own;" and he kisses her lips, unreproved.

"Then never doubt me, and always love me—if you can love the poor, faded old woman I am. But don't ask me to be your wife any more, James, for I cannot. How could I meet my father if I forgot this charge? I fear sometimes that all this is my blame—that I might have saved her"— she trembled and clung to him—"and it terrifies me so to think it, dear—it almost breaks my heart; and oh! I must never, never again leave her for a moment. Oh, father, father, forgive your poor child! Oh, James, give me your love, and pity, and sympathy, for I need it sorely."

"Take comfort, Marian. You are not to blame in this, my poor child. What were you to do, stretched on your fever-bed?"

"No—not then. But I ought to have guarded against any possibility of ill. Oh, James, you don't know what such a charge is, and how terribly one suffers for any neglect or oversight. Only—thank Heaven! —I have found her again."

"Give me reason to thank Heaven, too— oh, dearest, and only love——"

"Hush! It cannot be. *I dare not!*"
And she placed her hand on his lips.

He could not but see how bitterly her
heart was torn to refuse him. He pressed
her hand to his lips in one long kiss, and
sighed to think that the one vision of his
life was as far from him as ever.

But he could not refrain from returning
to the subject again and again. He be-
sought her for pity's sake to be his wife—
for the sake of her sister, who should be his
sister. But she would not listen to his
entreaties.

She could not divest her mind of the
belief that she might have averted the evil
which had befallen Alice. Nothing could
convince her that she had not in some way
neglected the solemn charge which devolved
upon her at her father's death.

In vain poor Mrs. Warner exercised all
her homely logic in pleading James's cause.
She could prosper little. And what defeated
them both was Marian's honest avowal of
her love for James.

"I shall never know what happiness is
except as his wife, Mrs. Warner, and yet I
know that cannot be. Duty is stronger
than love, and, if it breaks my heart, I must

obey my conscience. And my conscience tells me, too, that if I loved him, I should not bring the blemish of this shame as my wedding portion. I know he is too noble and too good to care for it himself; but I must think of him, and I know how such a disgrace would be told to his discredit in the world. No man who rises as he has done by his own merit is without enemies, and is it for me to supply them with stones to hurl at his fair name? It's breaking my heart, Mrs. Warner; and you're breaking it the faster to make me talk about it. But I tell you it must not and cannot be!"

And Mrs. Warner felt it was useless to argue with her any longer. Indeed, she felt that what Marian said about the use James's enemies might make of poor Alice's misery was too serious to be set aside lightly. She had lived long enough in the world to know how ready a man's foes are to stab him in the back, and distort a story that should be to his honour into a means of disgracing him.

Dreary, dark November was drawing to an end. All through the weary weeks the doctor and Death had been fighting a sharp battle over the patient's bed. Alice was seemingly better and stronger, but the doctor's expression had not worn away yet. Indeed, his anxiety was becoming more intense, for just as he was making a little way, the winter was coming on to undo all his work. For Alice's lungs were affected, and the weather-wise prophesied a bitterly cold December; and the doctor trembled for his patient.

December came; and for once the weather-wise were not out in their calculations. It opened with a bitter, black frost, that killed at once any lingering remnants of summer that had escaped the November fogs. When Marian or Mrs. Warner—for they took it by turns to sit up with the invalid now—used to steal across the room in the early dawn and look out of the window, the panes would be covered with the fantastic tracery of frost, and all the moisture of the night would glitter, transformed into miniature diamonds, on the window ledge and the flower pots. The roads even looked white sometimes, as if there had been a fall of snow.

Then Alice began to fade again, and her cough grew more hollow. They all trembled at the sound of it, it seemed to shake her poor frail body so terribly. There was no being blind to the anxiety in the good doctor's face now.

" What do you think, doctor ? " said Marian in a whisper.

" We must take care, Miss Carlyle. Do you think you could bear travelling ? " he said, turning and speaking very gently to Alice.

" I feel very weak," was all she could murmur.

" I think we ought to send her to Madeira ; at all events, to a warmer climate."

Mrs. Warner was showing him out as he said this, and he had nearly reached the door, which opened into the sitting-room where James Trefusis was waiting to hear his opinion of the invalid. Marian was sitting by Alice's bedside, with the poor bony hand clasped in hers.

" You think a warmer climate advisable, doctor ? What do you say to Cornwall ? I have long wished Miss Carlyle to accept a comfortable house in a snug valley in that delightful county. I have placed it at her disposal for some considerable period, but she does not avail herself of my offer."

The doctor turned to Marian as he stood in the doorway.

"It would be just the thing. I fear she could hardly bear the sea-passage, and she might be taken to Cornwall very easily. Pray go."

He spoke very earnestly. James had hardly made the proposal seriously, but was taking advantage of the opportunity to urge his suit. But the doctor evidently thought very highly of the suggestion.

"If you think so, doctor," said Marian, "and Mr. Trefusis will lend"—a slight emphasis on lend—"me the house for a time, we will go there. When should we start?"

"As soon as possible."

"But the house is not ready for habitation, perhaps?"

"It soon shall be, though," said James. "I'll go to Totting, my lawyer, this very moment, and order him to turn that scamp Cormack out at any cost, without a moment's delay."

"Stop!" said Marian hastily, in a strange tone of voice, from her seat by the bedside. "Don't go until I have seen you. Good-bye, doctor. Just leave us a moment, Mrs. Warner—and close the door!"

Marian had felt Alice shudder at the mention of Cormack's name, and a terrible suspicion had risen in her mind. She had never asked her sister for the story of her sufferings and shame; but now she must ask that one question.

What passed in that closed chamber, when the two sisters were left together alone, what need to tell ? Indeed it would be beyond my poor power to describe the harrowing scene. For then and there, unasked, as soon as the door was shut, Alice poured forth the long tale of her wrong and misery ; and the two wept on each other's shoulders, and mourned and prayed.

All this time James Trefusis sat in the next room, wondering what had chanced and what was to happen. He felt that it must have been something very strange that had made Marian speak as she did. He could hear the two sisters sobbing now, and he began vaguely to discern what was coming.

Presently the door opened, and Marian, with a face as white as a ghost's, came in. She sank into a chair by his side, buried her face in her hands, and remained silent for a minute or so. At last, in a low, gasping voice, she repeated to him what she had just learnt from Alice.

When she finished her recital, she looked up, and then shrank back, terrified at the fury she saw in James's face.

He rose from his chair without speaking a word, snatched up his hat, and taking his stick with a fierce grip as if he were clutching some one by the throat, hissed out, " Cormack shall suffer for this, if I live, by God !" And the imprecation was pardonable if ever one was, for his heart was bursting, and he was terribly—solemnly in earnest.

CHAPTER XVI.

HOW THEY PUT THE ENGINE TO WORK AT WHEAL CORMACK.

CAPTAIN TREGENNA is up and stirring with the first streak of day. It is not the nicest time of year to set the engine to work, but Cormack will not wait till the spring. It is arranged that large bonfires shall be lighted if the weather is too cold. But it never is very cold, even on the moors, in Cornwall, lying, as it does, an isthmus between two vast bodies of water, and with the Gulf Stream almost washing its western promontory.

It appears as if the weather had specially favoured Wheal Cormack. The anxious eyes of Captain Tregenna, watching the chill dawn, detect certain yellow rays that foretell the sun; and presently that luminary rises, and sheds almost summer warmth on the scene. It is a splendid morning. How lovely the moorland looks stretching away on all sides, with here and there a trail of vapour lingering by some stream or over a hollow. Beyond all is the pale blue sky, where the sun is climbing, red through the mists—but not so red as to portend a bad day. Captain Tregenna is delighted beyond measure. He had been so afraid something must occur to mar the great event of his life. The weather had been very unsettled of late, and he would have been little surprised if the dawn had broken luridly through curtains of rain. He had quite expected it, in fact, and had wondered whether the tents would keep out the wet, or whether the showers would be so heavy as to extinguish the fires.

All the village is on the move early, for the men have to help in making preparations for the reception of the guests. There must be stables extemporised in the workshops, and some sort of covering for the gigs and coaches in case it should rain. And those who have no work to do go to look on; and the women loiter about, ready to make themselves generally useful.

There is the putting up of evergreens, and the washing of all the plates, dishes, knives and forks that can be collected for the occasion ; and there is cooking on a large scale. How busy they all are !

Wheal Cormack resembles nothing so much as an ants' nest, the interior workings of which have been suddenly revealed by a chance footstep. There is an apparently aimless rushing to and fro, and eventual harmony and order emerging unexpectedly from chaos.

Henry Cormack comes over early to see how affairs are progressing, and he and Captain Tregenna are as jolly as sandboys, all is going so well.

The chief object of all this bustle meanwhile stands calm and stationary. The tall white engine-house, with the black beam of the engine thrust out like a giant arm, is motionless and deserted by all save the engineer, who is engaged inside furbishing up the brass, or wiping the rods of his charge with little bits of oily rag—taking that peculiar affectionate delight in retouching and finishing off that a young husband takes in setting his wife's bonnet ribbon aright, or altering the folds of her shawl.

The engine-house is a tall rectangular

building, with a lofty chimney. It is built with one floor, beneath which there are odd nooks and corners for stowage away of engineering odds and ends. From this floor to the roof the interior is occupied by the engine, one end of the beam—that which works the pumps in the shaft—protruding through an opening at the back of the building. Above this opening is a half-deck sort of floor, with a gallery outside, reached from the interior by a set of steps, which is something more than a ladder, and something less than a flight of stairs.

To the traveller in the mining districts, these engine-houses present a curious sight at night. The engines are always at work, and as you see one of these buildings looming dark against the midnight sky, with the great beam plunging and rising incessantly, it is almost impossible to avoid thinking of them as living creatures. They do their work so quietly when apparently all human labour has gone to rest. They seem like huge giants working at some vast sawpit.

The giant of Wheal Cormack was a sleeping giant as yet. The first downthrust of his arm on this day was to be the signal for great rejoicing; and when once he had fairly begun his monotonous labour, the good speed of the mine was to be a certainty. No wonder that so many anxious looks were turned to the engine-house this morning.

The guests are beginning to arrive. They have come long distances for mthe ost part. But in this county, whither the railway has not yet brought a distinct estimate of distance, people think nothing of driving twenty miles to dinner—and over such roads ! It will be a miracle, supposing the night turns out a little dark, and the sitting late and merry, if half of these people get home without something like an accident. For some part of the way they have to drive over the turf, for there is no road across the moor to the mine except that used by the ore waggons, and that is ploughed into ruts as big as young rivers. And the turf of the moor is not like the turf of a bowling-green. There are great ledges and reefs and boulders of granite sprinkled about it, and there are plenty of holes where they have been digging for gravel or water, or where some one has been prospecting. It must do old Doctor John's heart good, as he jogs over to the feast on his old white horse, to see

III.   Q

what odds there are in favour of an inquest. He is safe enough. He knows every inch of the moors, drunk or sober—that is to say, in the former case the old horse knows what he is about, and will carry him home all right.

It is a very miscellaneous collection of vehicles. Flies, dog-carts—not many of those, though—gigs, buggies, carts, and covered vans. And the horses are remarkable for a similar variety. There is the squireen's clever hack, and the mining captain's broken-kneed nag, and the post horse and the plough horse, and the horse that is only fit for the knacker's.

And if the vehicles and animals must be exonerated from the charge of a monotonous sameness, their owners or hirers—as the case may be—are just as heterogeneous an assemblage. Everybody who had ever dabbled in mines—and who had not?—at all events, everybody who might dabble in mines—and who might not?—had been invited to be present. And very few who were invited failed to come; even some who were not invited asked themselves.

There is a little body of grandees — the mining aristocracy—to whom Captain

Tregenna and Cormack pay deferential attention, and no one feels the least hurt or jealous at the preference so displayed. The fortunate speculators are the representative men of the class assembled here. There is no man in the throng who may not, and does not hope, to arrive at the same pinnacle of eminence. Each one, therefore, respects a position which he dreams he may some day acquire for himself.

*　　　*　　　*　　　*

What scheme of retribution James Tre-fusis proposed to himself when he left London with the intention of calling Cormack to account, I do not know. He probably did not know himself. His was the instinctive impulse to punish, and he hurried out of Marian's presence, and set forth westward without a moment's delay.

As the railway bore him along to Ply-mouth, he did not reflect on what course he should take. He simply revelled in the speed with which steam was taking him to the man he so hated.

From Plymouth he went on by the mail. What a delicious mode of travelling it was! —with four sturdy gray nags stepping out gloriously, and the guard's bugle waking the echoes! The jingle and rattle of the chains and swingle-bars made pleasant music, and how freshly the air rushed against the face! James enjoyed the speed here too, and checked off the milestones as they passed, thinking how rapidly his road was shortening—never thinking what he should do when his journey was accomplished.

At last the mail stops to change at the town whence James must post to Polvrehan. It is a quiet little country town, some eight miles from Polvrehan—but it seems more than ordinarily quiet to-day. James goes to The Bell to ask for a conveyance.

" Can I have a trap to——"

" Go over to Cap'n Cormack's ? " says the hostler; " not for love nor money, sir."

This startles James for a moment. How can the man guess his destination so readily? But the continuation of the hostler's speech explains it.

" If you'd a-come by the morning mail, you might ha' had a seat along with some of the others. There was one to spare in Mr. Cargill's fly. Know Mr. Cargill, sir ? "

" No, he does not," James says.

"Ah! But I dare say it wouldn't a-mattered, you being a friend of Cap'n Cormack, and invited, you see, sir—and I s'pose come from London a-purpose."

"On purpose for what?" James asks.

"Oh, I thought as you was going over to the dinner at Wheal Cormack to-day, sir. They're putting the new engine to work, sir. And a'most every one's invited, and I don't believe there's a horse and trap left in the place."

Still, without reflecting how he should visit Cormack with his revenge, James feels that this opportunity — this hour of his triumph—is the time to take advantage of. He asks, "Is there no saddle horse to be had?" The ostler says "Yes; but that, as the gentleman probably doesn't know his way across the moors, that wouldn't be much use."

James assures him he need not trouble about that; he knows all the moors about Polvrchan very well, and tells him to saddle the horse and bring it round.

As he waits on the steps of the hotel, his attention is attracted by a saddler's window on the other side of the road. He crosses over, and, after looking in for a short time, goes in, and buys a heavy hunting-crop —a tremendous weapon, with a hammer-head.

By the time he has completed his purchase he hears the clatter of hoofs outside, and sees his horse being brought round. So he goes out; mounts, and rides off to the moors.

*   *   *   *

Captain Tregenna and Henry Cormack are pointing out what a view there is from the gallery of the engine-house to a little knot of guests. They are waiting for the first movement of the engine.

It comes at last. The heavy beam oscillates for a moment, and then gives a downward plunge. There is a loud cheer. The beam rises again, and the rush of water in the launder (or channel from the pumps) tells that all works well.

"You're a little late, sir, whoever you are," says Cormack, as, looking away from the now steadily-working beam, he happens to catch sight of some one spurring across the moor towards the mine.

Bump !

One or two of the guests who have not been present on occasions of this sort look alarmed, and hurry downstairs, to the great amusement of the others, who know the meaning of the blow that made the engine-house shake.

It is the custom, when starting an engine for the first time, to play off this mild practical joke. The engineer "brings her home," as he calls it—that is, he lets the upward stroke of the beam continue until it strikes against the floor and gallery with a bang that startles the new comers, and affords considerable amusement to the old stagers.

" Bring her home again, lad," says the stoker.

" Aye, be sure," says the engineer.

Bang ! goes the engine, and the whole place quivers at the blow.

One or two of the old stagers begin to think the house is a little shaky. Some few of them know how lightly it has been run up, so there is a quiet move towards the stairs. Tregenna sees it, and begins to joke about it. The others hesitate, and the Captain, slipping by, runs down to the engineer, and tells him to " bring her home again ! "

Bang ! a third time. A slate falls off the

roof, and goes down outside with a crash, and some of the mortar falls rattling on the floor. The knot of guests upstairs don't delay now. They hustle each other most unceremoniously in their hurry to get out of the building. Cormack laughs at them, but he does not feel comfortable. As soon as they are outside, he goes to the side of the half-deck floor, whence he can see Tregenna, and shouts out, " Stop that infernal nonsense, Tregenna! Don't be a fool! "

But Tregenna had noticed nothing of the causes that sent the alarmed guests helter-skelter, and he is so intensely enjoying the joke that he has told the engineer to bring her home with a will once more.

Bang! At the same moment Tregenna hears Cormack's shout. He looks up. There is a crash and a dull rattle, and then the roof overhead suddenly yawns. It is all the work of a second. The engineer catches Tregenna by the arm, and drags him away through the door after the stoker, who fled at the first crash.

They are standing in the open air. There's a hollow rumbling and a cloud of dust. Then Tregenna is aware of the figure of the stoker struggling up from the ground.

He has been felled by a falling beam. Then he becomes conscious that he himself must have been struck by something on the left shoulder, for there is a sharp pain there, and he can't lift his arm.

What has happened? He is all confused, everything has passed so rapidly. He turns to look at the engine-house. It is gone. A cloud of dust is clearing away from a pile of stones and timbers, from the midst of which the engine-shaft rises, apparently uninjured, the beam still working, crushing up and down through the *débris*. Where is Cormack? He must be buried under the ruins.

" Come on, lads; we must get him out. Captain Cormack's buried in yon," he cries, shaking off his stupor.

He is about to spring forward; but a hand is laid on his shoulder. It is the engineer, who points to the tall chimney. There is a great gap at the bottom, where the brickwork has been torn down by the fall of the rest of the building. It looks as if the lofty shaft must fall at a breath of wind. It seems actually to totter as the beam—the steam not having been turned off by the engineer in his hurry—still crashes up and down in the ruins.

The peril is evident. No one dares to approach the ruins, for fear of the fall of the chimney. A dense ring gathers round the spot, but no one ventures within the circle, though every one is shouting, and ordering, and advising.

And what had all this seemed like to James Trefusis as he galloped across the moors?

He had seen the beam move, and heard the shout, and pushed on. Then something —he never could explain what, whether sight or sound — attracted his attention again; and then he beheld the heap of ruins, and the smoke of dust blowing away. He believed it was an explosion, but could not make out clearly. At any rate it was an accident, and a terrible one. For a time he forgot altogether the real cause of his coming, but spurred on with the instinct of a brave heart to go and offer aid under such a calamity.

In a few minutes he was bursting through the ring. One or two shouted out a warning to him that the chimney was likely to fall, but he took no heed. First of all he scrambled over the ruins, and thrust aside timber and rolled away stone with a fierce energy like a madman, until he could get at the engine to turn off the steam.

There were plenty of brave fellows in the crowd who only needed this amount of leading and example to make them face the danger without flinching. In another minute James was directing the operations of a dozen or more sturdy miners.

Nobody seemed to know how many were buried in the ruins, but they were not very extensive, and could be easily searched, provided the chimney did not fall. They toiled away with a will.

" There's an arm," cried somebody; and James was at the place in a minute, and an arm sure enough it was.

" Now carefully, lads. I'll get him out as gently as I can, if you'll remove the stone-work and that beam there. Carefully —take the stones off the top first. Gently ! Now, heave the beam—hold it up like that a bit, and I can ease him out." So shouted James, as, with the aid of Tregenna, he tenderly drew the man out of the ruins. He was lying on his face, with the beam across his back. As they lifted the balk,

James took him in his arms, and drew him out.

It was Cormack!

It was the man on whom James had vowed to be avenged. James Trefusis had him in his arms now—lifeless, motionless. And yet James Trefusis was actually trying anxiously to discover some signs of life in him, to find some hope of his return to consciousness. What strange creatures we are!

There's another warning shout now. The miners leap away, and Tregenna scrambles after them. James cannot, for Cormack lies a dead weight in his arms, and with such a burden, his footing on the ruins would be precarious. He looks up. It seems as if the tall chimney were curling over him. It falls; but fortunately it falls some yards on his left, so that, though he is struck by falling stones and flying rubbish, he escapes unhurt.

He carries the body of Cormack into the tent, and it is laid on the rough deal table at the head, which happens to be the nearest end to the engine-house. It was where the dead man would have sat, and where that famous speech of his was to have been made.

There are no speeches now, and the dinner is a mere necessary devouring of food by men who have come twenty miles from home. They must have something to eat—so they crowd into the lower end of the tent, so far away as possible from the cross table at the head. They snatch a hasty mouthful, and then traps are ordered out, and the party separates.

Doctor Johns has examined the body. Life is extinct. Cormack must have been killed almost instantaneously. The doctor is rather angry at this, for he would have had to attend Cormack if he had survived, and he feels done out of a patient as well as a dinner. So he drinks as much gin and water as he can with his hasty meal, and rides off home, disappointed, but not uncomfortable.

This was the day of Cormack's triumph —this was the day for James's revenge. And where was Cormack's triumph now? and what of James's revenge? Truly man proposes, but God disposes!

CHAPTER XVII.

AFTER STORM, CALM.

WHEN James returns to London, he finds that Alice has suddenly become worse, and is, in fact, as the doctor confesses to him, sinking fast.

He tells Marian this, but she still hopes that her sister may be spared. She tells Alice the story of Cormack's death as James told it to her.

"We all want to be forgiven, Marian, don't we?" says Alice.

"Much, darling, much," groans Marian, who, as we know, cannot forgive herself the evil which has befallen her sister.

"*I* forgive him. Will you?"

"Never! I cannot," says Marian, fiercely.

"Look at James, Marian. He would have saved his life if he could."

"No," says James, who has been sitting in the gloom on the other side of the bed.

"I did not know who it was until I drew him out of the ruins."

"But you would have done the same if you had known."

"I can't tell. I do not know. I went there perhaps to kill him myself."

"Thank Heaven you were not in time. Haven't I sins enough to answer for already?"

"Alice, darling, Alice, you must not talk so," says Marian, who knows that the doctor has forbidden Alice to speak much.

"I must and will talk," says Alice, vehemently, "for I see you are breaking James's heart, and all for me—wicked, bad me, that ought to be dead. Why didn't you let me die? There, I will speak," she says, sitting up and thrusting away Marian, who wishes to silence her. "I have lain here day and night thinking of it. You are breaking his heart, Marian, all because of me, and it makes me long to die."

Marian does not speak; she leans her head on her clasped hands, and weeps bitterly. She cannot tell Alice that what she says is not true—she cannot say that even were Alice herself dead, she could not consent to become James's wife because the shame would not be dead.

" Alice," says James, in a strange hollow voice, " neither you nor I can turn her. And if she does break my heart, it is her's, and has been ever since I was a lad. You must not make yourself unhappy because you think it is owing to your being here ill like this. We must all bear our bitter trials in this world, and this one is mine."

" But your's won't be the only heart that will break. Isn't her's breaking, too, James? Why, when I've been lying here, and she has thought me asleep, I have been watching her face—and if her heart is not breaking, never believe me, James; and I know what breaking hearts are, for I have seen them breaking many a time. Oh, James, save her from herself, and let me die in peace."

The strange feeling, that Alice was older than she was, came very strongly over Marian now. Once she had been used to pet and chide her sister—to regard her as a child. Now she listened to her sadly, solemnly, as to a woman. But still she remained firm to her purpose, though Alice renewed her entreaties again and again, while poor James sat by silent—but with a sad, grave face, whose eloquence was so touching and so hard to disregard.

Alice grew weaker and thinner every day. And her sufferings grew very terrible. But as the end drew near she was more peaceful in mind, for at first she had been almost frenzied with the horror of death—the death which she was seeking when Marian found her. Death had seemed a friend holding out his arms to her as she took the plunge from the dark bridge. Seated by her bedside, with his cold hand creeping quietly towards her heart, he seemed a cruel torturer. But in reality he was then her best friend; in the end she came to recognise him as such.

"Will it be long, doctor?" she began to ask. And the doctor would shake his head, and take her hand kindly.

"I've only one thing more to wish in the world, and then I could die happy, doctor. I might have that wish, might I not?"

"What is it?"

"Oh, it's a promise I want my sister to make. And she won't make it, and I lie

III. R

awake longing to hear her say ' Yes,' She might, might she not, doctor ? "

Alice repeated this so often that the doctor thought it worth his while to tell Marian.

" She will suffer fearfully before she dies —I mean physical pain, and so we must spare her all the mental agony we can. I don't know what this request is, but I suppose it is not a mere trifle, or you wouldn't refuse. But pray, Miss Carlyle, .see and think if you can't grant her request, for it is really preying on her mind."

But Marian shook her head, and said, " Impossible."

Still Alice's importunities became so earnest that the doctor was obliged to speak to James ; and James, in his turn, held a consultation with Mrs. Warner. That worthy woman had a keen judgment, and to her, moreover, Marian's confidences had been more unreserved. She gave it as her decided opinion that there was only one insurmountable barrier between Marian and James. The determination that she would not bring James the dowry of her sister's shame as her only dowry in the world, was strong and insuperable—all others might be overcome. And Mrs. Warner owned that she felt such an argument was not to be slighted, and she respected Marian's firmness on the point. James was a man whose position before the public would be assailed in every way by those who had failed where he had succeeded ; it would not be the part of a true wife to supply his enemies with weapons to injure him with.

James laughed at this reasoning, but he saw that Mrs. Warner was only repeating what was deeply rooted in Marian's mind.

" If that's all, I can remove that difficulty with great ease," he said, and smiled. But the smile was not without sadness, for the sacrifice he was about to make was no slight one. He had always taken a father's pride and interest in his invention. He had been constant to it in the days of its neglect, and he had become ardently attached to it now, and happy in its success. There was the natural pride of a man who has fought a long losing game, but has become victorious eventually by sheer pluck and self-reliance. He had worked and won, and the triumph was very pleasant to him. He was human—and, therefore, one ought not to be surprised that he found it delightful to

have the men who had slighted and in-
sulted him, now seeking him, cap in hand.

But this must all go now. He relin-
quished it—but not without a sigh.

A few evenings after his conversation with
Mrs. Warner, he and Marian are sitting
by Alice's bed—one on each side. She
is going very fast now, and her sufferings
are so acute that she cannot sleep, but lies
moaning uneasily.

"Give me your hand, Min—and yours,
James!"

They each gave her a hand, and she lies
quite still for a little while. Then she says,
"How dark it is! Oh, I do dread the long,
dark night! When will it be morning?"

James tells her it will not be dawn for
some hours; at which she sighs.

"Marian, I wish I might lay your hand
in James's, and leave it there—leave it
there for ever."

"Oh, hush, Alice, darling! It only
makes us all unhappy, and it must not be."

"I'm going to leave you, Marian; won't
you grant me this, for my peace?"

"I dare not!"

There is silence again for some time, and
then Alice moans:

"Oh, these weary, weary nights. How dark it is! Oh, for daylight—or sleep. Min, I could sleep better—I could sleep now—and I do so want to sleep—if I might join these hands."

But Marian shakes her head, sobbing bitterly.

"Listen, Marian, dearest," says James, in a low voice, as if not to disturb Alice, "would you marry me if I were a poor man again?"

"What use is it to ask that? This is idle talking, James."

"No, Marian, it is not idle talking. If I, James Trefusis, were the working man I was many years back, with nothing to rely upon but my sinews and my brains—a man going out to work his humble way in a new world, needing a wife to help and comfort him—would you say me no, Marian?"

"But it is not so; it cannot be so. If it were, you would not doubt my love—and yet I fear I might not be your wife."

"Not if I were going to a new country, where all would be strangers to us—a new country where we should be hundreds of miles from our nearest neighbours?"

"What do you mean?" asks Marian.

"If I were going to Australia, then, a poor labourer who has bought a little bit of land, and is going to settle on it, would you share my lot, or would you let me go out a lonely, friendless man, to grow gray in the solitudes, with no recollections of happy days—only a sad memory of one I loved"——

"And who loved you!" Alice broke in, softly.

"Am I dreaming, or is there some meaning in this?" Marian asks, faintly.

"Would you be my wife, then? Answer only in that one short word—yes or no."

"Yes!"

"Then Alice may lay your hand in mine for ever, dear wife, for I am that poor working man, going out to settle in Australia."

Alice clasped the two hands together, and raising them to her lips, kissed them with a long sigh of relief.

James explained that he had made over his invention to the old Captain of Artillery, to whom its origination was chiefly due, and that he had invested all his money in some land in Australia, which he intended to reclaim and cultivate himself.

There was great peace and a calm of happiness in that dark chamber.

" I shall be able to sleep now," said Alice. " Oh, Marian, this has filled my heart with comfort. Thank Heaven ! I shall be able to sleep now."

" Poor child," said James, " I hope you may, for you need rest."

" Oh, I feel I can sleep now—only let me hold your hands together like this. Kiss me, Marian."

Marian leant over and kissed her. Then they sat quite quiet, and listened to her breathing, which gradually became more regular, as if sleep were at last really coming to refresh her.

James and Marian sat thus for a long time. They did not need to speak, for they were communing in thought. Hand in hand, at last, plighted man and wife, whom nothing could part now, they sat in a waking dream of perfect content and peace. The only drop of bitterness in their cup was the certainty that poor Alice was dying, and that the path to their wedding lay across her grave.

They thought she was asleep, but presently she began to moan again :

"Oh, this weary, weary darkness! When will it be light?"

"Presently, darling; have patience."

She lay quiet for a time, and then said, "You won't deceive me, will you, Marian? It is not a plot of yours and James's to say this just to pacify me? You will be his wife?"

"I will, his faithful wife, please God," said Marian, solemnly.

"Call him 'husband,' then—just for once, that I may hear it."

"My husband," said Marian, lingering lovingly on the name.

"My own dear wife," said James, in a voice broken with emotion.

"Thank Heaven!" said Alice, "now I shall sleep."

She pressed their hands over her heart, and there was silence. At last she murmured faintly, "It is growing lighter now!" They believed she had fallen asleep. And she had fallen asleep indeed, and was not to wake again.

And so James and Marian were betrothed, and their united hands were laid upon a broken heart for an altar.

They sat all through the long hours of

night in this way, fearing to move lest they should disturb poor Alice's slumbers. But when the dawn broke, and they could see her face, they knew that the sleep she was sleeping was not to be broken by earthly noises. And Marian knew her sister was gone, and she flung herself into James's arms, and wept upon his shoulder. He led her away from the dead, until the first agony of her grief was over. Then he took her back to the bedside, and showed her what a calm, sweet smile there was on the face, and how it had lost the worn and wasted look, and seemed young and fair once more.

"That is peace," he whispered. And Marian felt it was peace, and her grief was comforted somewhat, for that bitterness of death which she had feared had been spared to that unhappy sister of hers—and of us all !

CHAPTER XVIII.

"TILL DEATH DO US PART!"

SPRING at last! The long weary winter was over, and nature was waking from her sleep. There were clumps of primroses in sheltered nooks, and the osier beds were gay with golden catkins. The woods were just brightening with the early leaf buds, and the colour of the springing corn was discernible in a faint film of green on the fields. The birds began to sing in the hedgerows, and the lambs skipped merrily in the pastures.

And in a very few days how the tiny green buds swelled and opened into little leaves, and how rapidly the little leaves grew and spread as the sap coursed along. You could almost see the green fans of the horse-chestnuts grow as you watched them.

The fields were so fresh and bright with

the young grass. Here and there you saw little patches that seemed to have borrowed their colour from the clear skies above—but it was only the bluebells. The graceful ferns put forth their quaint clubs, like augurs' staffs, foretelling summer.

Every now and then the air would darken, and there would be the sudden whispering of showers among the leaves, but they did not last long. Away sailed the watery cloud, often with a rainbow fringing its skirts, and then all around would twinkle with the lavish diamond-drops. And for every shower that obscured the heavens for a space, there would come greener leaves, and taller stems, and bigger blossoms, so that you almost loved to hear the pattering of the rain for the sake of the store of loveliness it was laying up for to-morrow.

It was April—the real spring month, when all the most wonderful phenomena of Nature's re-awakening are to be observed. March is the babyhood of the year. It lies helpless almost in the arms of winter, and if it were not for the violets that are its eyes, you would think it was asleep. But April is the childhood of the year, with all its smiles and frowns, developing fresh

traits, and displaying new powers and intelligence every day, as children do.

It is April, that comes in with a handful
of primroses, and leaves behind it cowslips
and cuckoo-flowers as a remembrance. April
always reminds me of Ophelia—laughter in
tears, tricked out with pretty wreaths and
flowery fancies.

In speaking of Spring and April, I find
I have wandered into a description of their
beauties as displayed in the country. But
it is not of the country that I am about to
write.

Spring and April visit the humble suburb
where the church and school of St. Pacifica
preside over modest tenements and "eligible
sites for building." There is a pleasant
odour of lilacs on the air, and here and
there a laburnum begins to hint at the
showers of gold it will droop with by-
and-by.

During the winter the male denizens of
this quiet suburb have been compelled to
give up their sederunts in shirt-sleeves and
back gardens. There has been no clinking
about of pattens in the yards, for the washes
have all been dried indoors, filling the
habitations with a satisfying warm steam

that makes the babies, where there are babies in the case, assume the appearance of a well-cooked potato.

It has been hard times in many of these little dwellings. The winter is a sore trial for the struggling poor. Things are dear, and there is not much work to be had, and coals rise every week, but have to be bought every week as a rule nevertheless, for the want of a little capital to invest in a small stock. What is worse, where some extra prudent wife has, with a view to the washing she takes in, put by a little store of money to get in a ton, the chances are she has been cheated out of it. A handsomely dressed and civil spoken gentleman, with a flower in his button-hole, and his hat very much on one side, has paid a polite visit, and declared himself to be the agent of some large and well-known firm of coal merchants. He has, so he says, orders to come round with a view to accommodating small purchasers who can't buy when coals rise, and he is prepared to send in a ton— even less—of the best coals at a mere nominal sum, it being autumn, and large supplies looked for from the mines. And perhaps the poor woman is deluded into

ordering some; and if she pays the gentlemanly traveller for them on the spot, sees
no more of him from that day forth; but if
she undertakes to pay on delivery, she finds
when the money has gone, and the man
who brought the coals has gone, that she
has been supplied with an article which
would be invaluable if she wanted to re-
slate the roof, but is quite useless as fuel.

So what with hard times and dishonest
times, April is very welcome when it brings
sunshine to the struggling neighbourhood of
St. Pacifica's.

The shirt sleeves appear in the back
garden, but take to active occupations—
digging, hoeing, and raking. The back
gardens become netted across and across
with twine, as if the dwarf walls were
playing at cat's-cradle. But it is only a
provision for expected scarlet-runners. A
great deal of trouble is taken to adorn the
beds with fluttering rags of bright cloth
tied to sticks of firewood. This is done in
the fond belief that it will deter the sparrows
from eating the seeds. It is a vain delu-
sion. The London sparrow is too familiar
with man to be frightened at a scarecrow—
much less at a shred of cloth. You might

as well try to frighten a London street boy with the threat of a policeman. The cats, who have begun, now that April has come, to bask on the walls once more, must exercise all their cunning to catch Master Sparrow. As for the mongrel dogs, who always watch their master's digging, with an air of intense wonder at such unusual energy, they may bark at the sparrows when they see them picking all the beans out of the ground, but the bold birds don't care. If the cur runs at them, they just fly another foot from him, and begin gardening again.

The field which lies adjacent to the school-yard, having probably never seen such a thing as a primrose for years, does not attempt to mark spring in that way. But the turf, which is rather threadbare and out at elbows, like the best suits in the neighbourhood, tries to keep up an appearance, and is really green in places. The four daisies and the twelve dandelions which adorn it, do their best to impress you with the notion that there are flowers about. The sticklebacks in the stagnant pools are in full force, giving great sport. They bite tremendously, and expert fishermen are reported to have caught as many as six in half an hour—not to mention three more which were jerked out of the water, but dropped off.

One day in April there is great excitement at St. Pacifica's. The schoolroom is like a garden, so full is it of all sorts of early flowers. The children are to have a holiday and a great treat. Some of the more bold and enterprising spirits hang about the school and snatch furtive peeps of the interior arrangements. Tommy Wiggles declares—and is prepared to make that declaration on oath—that he saw a plum cake on the table as large as the top of his (Tom Wiggles's) mother's copper. This statement, I am bound to admit, is not received unreservedly by the youth of St. Pacifica's. Nor does Billy Darke, whose brother is apprenticed to Mr. Bocking, the baker, and who alleges on that brother's authority that penny buns have been ordered in by the gross, obtain much credence. It is whispered that he has invented the story in order to draw attention to the fact that his brother is in daily contact with penny buns, and possibly even with raspberry three-corners. There is no doubt about the

three large black kettles, because they were
seen going in; and indeed the handles of
two of them, together with part of their
spouts, are visible to the naked eye as they
stand in the window seat. A concourse of
mugs, and one of the largest assemblages
of plates on record in the parish, have also
been marked down as arriving at the school-
house.

A large barrel of beer has arrived, and
also a few bottles of spirits, by special per-
mission of the Reverend Augustus Rudgeworth, who explains to James Trefusis that
he despises the teetotal movement, and
places no faith in gentlemen who bandage
themselves with blue ribbon, and make a
special glory of practising one out of many
virtues which are simply the duties of every
man. But the Rev. Augustus Rudgeworth
does not wish to encourage drinking, and is
very severe on the point of rum as a substitute for milk, disapproving strongly of
tea being considered—as it is by a good
many of the female population hereabouts
—in the light of a vehicle for the best
Jamaica.

There is to be a tea for the children and
their fathers and mothers, with a magic

III.   S

lantern and some fireworks in the evening. And as Peggy Dobbs, who owes his name Peggy to the fact that one of his legs is of wood, is invited, the general belief goes that there may be a dance. For Peggy Dobbs, having no children, can have no claim to be asked, except that he plays on the fiddle; an accomplishment he acquired in the navy, where he lost his leg—not in action, but by tumbling down the hold with a barrel of salt pork.

"And the occasion," you ask, "of all this?"

Don't ask me. Ask one of those happy-looking youngsters—so happy that they don't mind having clean faces, even to the extent of a high soapy polish.

"Oh, if you please, Teacher's going to be married!"

Yes, James and Marian are to wed this bright April morning. April, the delightful month, when sun and shade mingle—when storm and sunshine alternate, as they do in our lives—is the fittest month of all for a marriage. There is no truth in the old rhyme—there seldom is any soundness in old proverbs—about the happiness of the bride on whom the sun shines. Not a bit of it: the sun can't always shine. The happiest bride must learn that the most blessed wedded life is April weather. Let her take shower and shine together on the one day of her life that she will remember till her dying hour—every incident of which, every glimmer of sunlight, every twinkle of rain-drop, shall be clear in her memory, until the loosening of the silver cord and the breaking of the golden bowl.

As they walk to church, the rich incense of grateful earth, returning thanks for a bounteous shower, fills the air with sweetness. But the sun is out, and the only drops that fall are flashing diamonds, that glitter brightly on the eaves before they drop to earth.

It is a very humble wedding. Mrs. Bartlett and Mrs. Warner accompany Marian; her bridesmaids are her three oldest pupils at St. Pacifica's. They are all dressed very nicely, but very quietly. Marian has a plain straw bonnet, with a white ribbon, a fawn-coloured shawl, and a dove-coloured silk dress. She might be a Quakeress, so simply is she attired.

James goes to church with Charlie Crawhall; and the old Captain of Artillery is to give away the bride. James is looking

almost young again; and when Marian,
coming in, sees him standing at the altar
steps, she thinks that he never looked so
tall before.

The Reverend Augustus Rudgeworth is
to perform the ceremony.   He is not "assisted" by anybody, though I believe he
needs it more than a good many of the
reverend gentlemen who require the aid of
two or three brother clerics to get through
the service, if the marriage announcements
in the *Times* mean anything. The Reverend
Augustus Rudgeworth is very much affected,
and nearly breaks down, for Teacher was a
great favourite of his, and he knows when
she is married she is to go away from them.
Marian has been a long time at the school,
and is greatly beloved.   Old pupils, who
have left long since, and who are married
or in service, come to see Teacher's wedding, and cry their eyes out in their simple
way, as if she were condemned thereby to
utter misery, instead of fulfilling the one
hope of her life.

In spite of chokes and coughs, which are
sobs in another form, the Reverend Augustus
Rudgeworth reads the noble service very
impressively: and there is only one mis-

take throughout, and that is committed by James, who apparently is so eager to assert his determination to make Marian his wife, that he says " I will !" with great emphasis directly the Reverend Augustus Rudgeworth asks him if he will have her for his wedded wife, and without waiting until he has completed the sentence. Nobody smiles, however, for there is something too solemn in the occasion. These two people are not children, uniting their fortunes blindly. James's hair is grizzled, and there are silver streaks in Marian's smooth plaits. A man and woman who have loved in spite of separation, and who have overcome all impediments — are about to join their lives — their hearts — their souls — their whole being. "Amen!" The ceremony is over.

The two bells of St. Pacifica's begin to ring like mad. They tinkle away at express speed, under the impression that careless observers may take them for a peal. And there is great rejoicing and hand-shaking, and then all adjourn to the schoolroom.

You see my people are humble people. I can't give you a breakfast from Gunter's, and therefore you must be content to sit

down in the school where Marian has
taught and laboured so long.

How happy everybody is till the time
comes for James and Marian to leave.
They are going down to dear old Cornwall
for a week, and then take ship for the New
World, where their future life lies.

" Good-bye—God bless you both ! " is all
that the Rev. Augustus Rudgeworth can
find power to say. And Charlie Crawhall
and the Captain wring James's hand in
silence, while Mrs. Bartlett and Mrs.
Warner are taking heart-breaking leave of
Marian.   And then the children have to
bid Teacher farewell; and during that she
fairly breaks down, for each of them has
some little speech, or promise, or memory
of old times for her.   Even Jack Banks,
the dunce of the school, who never could
master his " duty towards his neighbour,"
promises to struggle with that portion of
his Catechism till he gets it off, and says,
" when he's a man, he'll come over to
Horsetailor, and say it to Teacher."   So
farewell to all—from the biggest girl in the
school, Mary Middleton, who goes out to
service next week at a certain Mrs. Bartlett's, who is a good mistress, down to little

Polly Martin, who is too young to learn to spell, and is taught orally therefore, but cannot be persuaded that "forgive us our grasshoppers" is not a passage of the Lord's prayer.

"Good-bye all! And now I am yours, James! A poor gift, my darling," and she looks up tenderly in his face and he strokes her head. "Ah, James, it is a silver head——"

"But a golden heart!" he breaks-in, "A golden heart, tried and fined again and again in the fierce furnace of tribulation, but true gold!"

"It is all yours, James!"

So she goes away on her husband's arm, smiling through her tears on this April day, when all trace of Marian Carlyon is lost, but the world is blest with a Marian Trefusis.

CHAPTER XIX.

THE CLEARING.

I AM drawing near that inevitable line which must be the last boundary of every story. I have to dismiss my people, not without regret, for I have grown to feel an interest in every one of them—even the worst. Let us take a glance at the list of *dramatis personæ*, and see what becomes of them.

There was an inquest, of course, on the body of Henry Cormack, at Wheal Cormack, with the intelligent and experienced Mr. Lusky as foreman, and they brought in a verdict of " Accidental death," combined with a censure on " the person concerned in the erection of the engine-house and engine "—which, in point of fact, was a censure on the deceased, only Dr. Johns did not discover it.

Mr. Creech, Cormack's solicitor, an-

nounced that there was no will. A draft
had been prepared, but had not been
executed. Who was to have the property?
Cormack, you remember, was one of those
men who appear to spring up spontaneously
—who have no father, mother, or relatives
—a " kindless villain." Creech advertised
for the next of kin, and two or three claim-
ants came forward; and there was liti-
gation in Chancery; and, finally, what was
got over the devil's back was spent under
his belly — in other words, the lawyers
sacked the ill-won estate.

The Foundry passed into the hands of a
Joint-Stock Company (Limited). Shares
in the Polvrehan Ironworks and Steam
Foundry are, I see by to-day's *Times*, at a
premium. A large mining company has
sprung up on the moors; " Wheal Cor-
macks " are quoted at fabulous prices; and
there are several other dividend-paying
mines in its immediate vicinity. Polvrehan
is the property of a gentleman from Salis-
bury, who is a great mining adventurer,
and has made a large fortune out of this
new district. He has enlarged the house
considerably, and has added a tower, which
you can see from one of the high viaducts

on the Cornwall Railway as you look up
the valley of the Rella.

Lord Lacquoigne, I grieve to say, appears
to be a very great invalid. He lives a
good deal abroad, and is almost forgotten
in society, but his name is to be met with
frequently in the advertisements of patent
medicines. It is from those sources that
I learn that, after five years of agony from
dyspepsia and nervous depression, his lordship was restored to health by taking
Puffin's Vegetable Pills; and that conges-
tion of the liver must have eventually
removed him from this world had not a
friend recommended him to try Crammer's
Ointment, which gave him immediate relief.
It is from these facts, as set forth in his
grateful testimonials to the efficacy of these
medicines (signed " Your obedt. servt., Lacquoigne "), that I gather he is an invalid.
He has suffered tortures from neuralgia,
until he resolved to try Bosher's Nervoleni-
tive. He has been unable to walk until
Baron Bounce extracted his corns; and (I
have a faint impression) after becoming
bald (in consequence probably of the pain
he suffered from his teeth or his toes), had
a fine crop of hair produced in a week by

Swindall's Formula. Rude people have told me that his lordship is in robust health, and never takes physic, but that he pens these testimonials " for a consideration; " but such an explanation is too wildly improbable. I fear there is more truth in the rumour that, the aristocratic nose having been brought to the grindstone by poverty, her ladyship is the author of the mysterious announcement that " a lady of title, moving in good society, will engage to introduce ladies and gentlemen into the first circles, etc., etc., etc." There are so many snobs dying to get into high life—so anxious to insinuate themselves among the swells— that they will pay any price to the person who will get the thin end of the wedge in for them. No doubt her ladyship, putting her aristocratic nose to that use, makes a fair amount of money.

Mrs. Orr has grown very fat and very pious. She has to be wheeled about in a Bath chair, from which she dispenses to passers-by, of whose lives and characters she knows nothing, agreeable tracts, which announce definitively that they are going to a warm climate—not in the Tropics—at express speed. She lives in good style, which her means, though comfortable, do not seem adequate to maintain. But it must be remembered she collects for charities, and is a treasurer of various funds, and, as she is very humble-minded now, that is profitable. For you see, when she gets a donation of ten pounds for a mission to convert the heathen, she has only in pious self-depreciation to look upon herself in the light of a heathen, and her claim to five pounds out of the ten is indubitable.

The Hon. Mrs. Henry Vorian is, so Mrs. Orr says, worldly and carnal-minded. She is very fond of Bath and Cheltenham, where she finds a certain sort of society which admits her. The pinkness of her eyes has extended to her nose now, which is very sharp and spiky. She likes curaçoa, but has been known in the absence of liqueurs (a thing not uncommon in her own establishment) to put up with the neat gin of her native land. For a time she tried to fascinate, but as the only conquest she made was an old Admiral with a gouty foot, who would take port wine, and having taken port wine would take liberties, which her sensitive nature was horrified at—he actually kissed her once, and wanted her to sit on the knee that wasn't gouty—she abandoned the notion, and went in for whist and tabbies.

Her son, who is spoilt by his mother and his grandmother, is a promising youth. He only resembles his father in the worst and weakest points of his character. When patent medicines can no longer snatch Lord Lacquoigne from the clutches of death, the Hon. Henry Orr Vorian will be raised to the peerage, of which he will doubtless become a distinguished ornament. The women have ruined him in the bringing up. He doesn't hunt, or shoot, or boat. He won't go to the University, or take a commission. He is simply a fast man about town—so fast that he may outstrip his Lordship, and die before him.

Of Major Cantlow the traces are not very easy to follow. After his disappearance from Boulogne, he is not to be found until he turns up as a fortunate speculator at Wiesbaden. A suspicion of his play in a game at *écarté* leads a young German to challenge him, and he is so pressing in his invitation that the Major can't get out of the difficulty except by calling in the police. He gets off fighting by this means, but has to leave Wiesbaden. From this time he turns up at intervals wherever billiard balls rattle or gold coins glisten on green cloth. Finally, he is seen in Paris, under the name of Captain Cantley, winning heavily at a gambling table in a house on one of the Quais. He leaves with a large sum in gold and notes, and from that day seems to have abjured play, for he is never seen again. But about this time, any one curious in these matters might have seen, in visiting the Morgue, the corpse of an elderly man, with an aqualine nose, and a long, gray moustache, a stony eye, and a pale complexion. There were no marks of violence observable on the body, as it lay on its back on the slab, with the cold stream of water trickling over it. But had you lifted it and turned it over, you would have seen a gaping gash—the mark of a stab with a poignard—under the left shoulder blade. It was found in the Seine. The pockets had been emptied, and there were no means of identification. But the porter of a lodging-house, missing a lodger, and, like a wise Parisian, dropping in here, recognised the English gentleman who lived *au second* at his house —" an ex-officer, Capitaine Cantley, of the Armée Britannique."

Mrs. Bartlett and Mrs. Warner have become fast friends, and have gone into partnership in a large private hotel in St. James's.

Mrs. Bartlett's old lodging-house in Duke-street has been taken off her hands by a gentleman who was " own gentleman " to a nobleman who had chambers there. My lord's gentleman retired from the proud occupation of waiting on his Lordship in order to marry Mrs. Bartlett's servant, Mary Middleton, and set up as lodging-house keeper.

Mrs. Bartlett and Mrs. Warner are making a great deal of money by their private hotel, which is admirably conducted. They have only had one unpleasantness since they opened it. A foreign gentleman and lady came to reside there—the Count and Countess de Varignan—but they had not been there a week before they were taken up for being concerned in the forgery of French notes. On the trial it came out that so far from being the Count and Countess of Varignan, they were mere adventurers, who were not even married. The man was transported; the woman, who turned Queen's evidence, was acquitted, but as she disappeared mysteriously soon afterwards, it was conjectured that some of the gang had taken vengeance on her for betraying them. She had at one time opened a bonnet-shop in Pimlico, under the name of Delamere, at which time she was living with the proprietor of a café in Soho. He got into difficulties, and left the country. Miss Delamere became bankrupt, and was lost sight of until she emerged as a full-blown countess.

I am glad to see it announced that the Bishop of London has given a city living value £400 per annum to the Rev. Augustus Rudgeworth. The Rev. Augustus is an enviably lucky man for a parson who hasn't a living in his family. He has only been a curate in the poor and populous parish of St. Pacifica's five-and-twenty years, so that this recognition of his deserts comes surprisingly early.

Bohemia and its inhabitants are where they were when first James Trefusis wandered into the kindly land. Radical and revolutionary in theory, Bohemia is conservative in practice. It goes on in the same way for ever, and its sons never seem to change or grow old. Charlie Crawhall still paints pictures, and plays on his colour harmonicon. Dr. Long still believes that his plan of trephining must eventually be adopted by the faculty, while Harry Ryder continues to add last touches to the great epic, " Cromwell." Groeller's opera is not accepted yet, but that is partly because he has not quite completed it. Kiste disappears now and then, as of old, and then drops in some quiet evening, and says he has been in Central Africa, or the interior of Australia, since he was there last. Mark Latrowe is illustrating " Blue Blazes Ben, or the Young Burglar," which is issued in weekly numbers, price one penny—" No. 1, with which is given away, gratis, No. 2, and a magnificent engraving of the boy burglars burning the police station, now ready!" Jack Latrowe, after a more than ordinarily audacious " do," retired from Bohemia, and is keeping an inn somewhere in the country.

And now I have but one thing more to show you. It is an Australian scene. There's a large clearing, in which are clustered log farm-buildings. There is a pleasantly prosperous look about it, and every one on the place seems happy and contented.

III.   T

It is called New Polvrehan, and the owner, Mr. James Trefusis, is a rich man. He has worked steadily, and fortune has smiled on him. He might return to England, if he chose, now, and live like a prince. But he does not care about returning to England. The years he passed there were years of doubt, and trial, and anguish. The years he has spent in Australia are years of unclouded sunshine. His children have sprung up around him, to make this little clearing in the wilderness a world for him.

You would hardly recognise our old friend James. He is sunburnt and sinewy, and looks ten years younger than when last we saw him. His wife is a plump, pleasant body, with a cheery voice that is always singing over the work. Time with her, too, seems to have put back the hands some years.

There are three girls—Alice, and Marian, and Hannah; and two boys, James and Charles.

It is April—but not Spring. The glories of autumn gild the scene. It is the peaceful close of the year; it is the calm fulness of middle age.

"Do you know what to-day is, dear?" says the plump little woman, looking up from the table on which she is laying out damper and tea.

"Tuesday, my lass."

"But the day of the month, James?"

"Our wedding-day, to be sure. Do you think I'd forgotten it? Not a bit—I've been thinking of it all day while I was out after the cattle. I've brought you something home as a present."

"What is it?" says Marian, wonderingly, for she knows there are no shops where presents could be got for many a score of miles.

"Come here and see."

She goes up to him, and he folds her in his arms and kisses her on the forehead.

"There, that's what I've brought you. Have you nothing for me?"

She reaches up, and kisses him on the lips.

Then Alice, their first-born, comes in—and, as by one impulse, they both go to her and embrace her. She is the only delicate child they have—but it is not on that account that they thus fondle her. The memory of a poor, broken heart, at rest

Highgate Cemetery, far away across the ocean, in old England, makes them regard their eldest child with more than ordinary tenderness.

. The other children come in, for the evening meal is ready, and the sun is setting. It is a peaceful autumn evening.

The bright rays of departing day brighten the scene. They touch Marian's locks, and transmute the silver of her hair to gold. But no sun, nor shade, nor trouble, nor happiness can transmute the golden heart that has been purified by affliction!

THE END.

WYMAN AND SONS, PRINTERS, GREAT QUEEN STREET, LONDON.

www.ingramcontent.com/pod-product-compliance
Lightning Source LLC
Chambersburg PA
CBHW031346070726
47496CB00017B/1794